Adventure Stories for
Ten Year Olds

Helen Paiba is known as one of the most committed, knowledgeable and acclaimed children's booksellers in Britain. For more than twenty years she owned and ran the Children's Bookshop in Muswell Hill, London, which under her guidance gained a superb reputation for its range of children's books and for the advice available to its customers.

Helen was involved with the Booksellers Association for many years and served on both its Children's Bookselling Group and the Trade Practices Committee. In 1995 she was given honorary life membership of the Booksellers Association of Great Britain and Ireland in recognition of her outstanding services to the association and to the book trade. In the same year the Children's Book Circle (sponsored by Books for Children) honoured her with the Eleanor Farjeon Award, given for distinguished service to the world of children's books.

She retired in 1995 and now lives in London.

Adventure

STORIES

for Ten Year Olds

COMPILED BY HELEN PAIBA

ILLUSTRATED BY DOUGLAS CARREL

MACMILLAN
CHILDREN'S BOOKS

For Carol Alexander with love and thanks HP

First published 2001 by Macmillan Children's Books
a division of Macmillan Publishers Limited
25 Eccleston Place, London SW1W 9NF
Basingstoke and Oxford
www.macmillan.com

Associated companies throughout the world

ISBN 0 330 39142 9

1 3 5 7 9 8 6 4 2

A CIP catalogue record for this book is available from
the British Library.

Typeset by SX Composing DTP, Rayleigh, Essex
Printed and bound in Great Britain by
Mackays of Chatham plc, Kent

Contents

Batty

Paul Jennings

A stone with a hole in it. A sort of green-coloured jewel in a leather pouch. Just lying there in the beam of my torch.

Someone must have dropped it. But who? There was only Dad and me and our two little tents, alone in the bush. I picked the pouch up by the piece of leather thong which was threaded through it. Then I crawled into my tent.

I should have shown Dad the stone with the hole in it. But he was snoring away inside his tent and I didn't want to wake him. And there was something odd about it. The pouch was worn and the thong was twisted. As if it had hung around someone's neck for many years.

Who was the owner? Who had lost it way out here in the wilderness?

I snuggled down inside my sleeping bag and hoped that no one was snooping around. The noises of the bush seemed especially loud. Frogs chirped in a billabong. "Well, *they* can't hurt you," I said softly.

Something bounded through the scrub. "Kangaroo," I whispered to myself.

A growling grunt filled the night air. "Koala," I thought hopefully.

I closed my eyes and tried to make sleep come. I dared not listen to the rustlings and sighings outside. I told myself that Dad's tent was only a few metres away. But in that dark, dark night it could have been a million miles.

Scared? I was terrified. What if someone was out there? Creeping. Watching. Waiting. "Get hold of yourself, girl," I said to myself. "There is no one out there."

A twig broke. Snapped clean in the night. I stopped breathing. I stopped moving. But I didn't stop thinking. "Go away. Please go away," begged my frozen brain. I wanted to call out to Dad but my mouth wouldn't work.

The flap of the tent lifted. I could see the stars and the black trees. Someone moved. A shadow rustling, searching. Hands took my bag and opened it. I wanted to cry out but something stopped me.

Two pinpoints of light moved in a dark head. Eyes. Desperate eyes.

Quietly I moved my fingers. Like a spider's legs

they crept under the blankets towards my torch. "Softly, don't disturb him. Don't make him angry." With shaking hands I pointed the torch into the gloom. I felt like a soldier with an empty gun. I flicked on the switch.

And there he was. A wild boy with tangled hair and greasy skin. He was covered in flapping rags.

The tent was filled with a terrible squeaking like a million mice.

The boy reared back. In one hand he held a piece of cake from my bag. And in the other was the pouch with the hollow stone. He sucked in air with a hiss, turned to flee and then stopped.

He looked at me with a silent plea. A desperate call for help. He held his hand in front of his face to stop the light of the torch. The moon escaped from a bank of clouds and softened the tent with light. I should have called for Dad. But my eyes were locked in silent conversation with the intruder.

I could see that the boy was as frightened as me. He was poised to run. Like a wild animal wanting food but unable to take it from a human hand. I had to be careful. A wrong movement and he . . .

"Hey," yelled Dad.

It was just as if someone had turned out a light. The boy vanished in a twinkle. I didn't even see him go.

Dad and I sat up nearly all night talking about what had happened.

It seems that a hermit called Lonely Pearson had once lived out here in a hut with his wife and son. The wife was an expert on bats, like Dad. Nine years ago she died and Lonely became enraged with grief.

Lonely did some mean things. He burned every-thing that belonged to her. Her books, her clothes, her photos of the bats. The lot. It was almost as if he was angry with her for dying and leaving him alone with the little five-year-old son – Philip.

The only thing that was left was a green stone with

the hole in it. Philip's mother had always worn it round her neck. He used to play with it while she read him stories at bedtime.

After she died Philip hid the stone. Lonely Pearson ranted and raved. He shouted and searched. He nearly tore their hut to pieces. But Philip wouldn't show him where it was. He closed his mouth and refused to speak. He kept his secret and Lonely never found the stone.

"So what happened to Philip?" I asked Dad.

"He ran off into the bush. Lonely couldn't find him. No one could find him. The police searched for weeks and weeks. Then they gave up. Everyone thought he was dead."

I took a deep breath. "What about Lonely?" I said.

"He spent every day searching for his son. He never gave up. Lonely died last year."

I couldn't stop thinking about that sad, bewildered face staring at me in the moonlight.

"How can he live out here?" I asked. "It gets really cold at night. And there's nothing to eat."

Dad shook his head and turned down the kerosene lamp. "That's enough for tonight," he said. "You go to sleep. We have two days of climbing before we reach the bat cave. You are going to need all the rest you can get."

"But . . ." I began.

"Good night, Rachel."

I heard him zip up his sleeping bag. I was in Dad's tent. It was a bit of a squash but Dad thought it was safer.

"Good night," I mumbled. I was thinking about the next night. I was going back to my own tent. I had no doubts about that.

The next day was hot and our packs were heavy. Dad and I struggled through the dense bush. Down into wet gullies filled with tree ferns and leeches. Up dry, rocky slopes through sharp, scratching thorns. Along trails where kookaburras called and cicadas filled the air with chirping.

It was wonderful country but my pack was heavy. And so was my heart. There was a sadness in the air. At times I thought I glimpsed a hidden watcher. But I could never be quite sure. I would turn quickly. A branch moved slightly. Or did it?

We stopped for lunch in a mossy glen. Dad passed me a piece of cake. It was starting to go stale. I wrapped it up and put it in my pocket.

"Not hungry?" asked Dad.

"I'm keeping it for later," I replied. I was too. But not for me. I had plans for that bit of cake.

We packed up and moved on. Sometimes we went up. And sometimes down. But we were getting higher and higher.

My dad was a greenie. And of all living things he loved bats best. He was mad about them.

We were heading for a bat cave in the mountain's highest tops, Bat Peaks. Dad was going to block off the entrance to the cave. The roof was beginning to fall in. If it collapsed, the whole colony of bats would be destroyed.

"But they will all starve," I had said when he first told me the plan.

"No," he had replied. "We block the cave entrance at night. When they are out feeding. They will be forced to find another cave. It's the only way to save the colony."

So there we were. Trudging up the mountain. On our way to blow up a bat cave before it collapsed and killed the bats.

Dad had bats on his brain. But all I could think of was a boy called Philip.

That night we camped in a forest clearing. Our camp fire crackled between a circle of stones. Overhead the stars filled the cold night like a handful of sugar thrown at the sky. It didn't seem as if there could be anything wicked in the world.

The gums were ghostly and grey. The ground was home to pebbles and thorns and ants. I shuddered at the thought of someone living out there. Barefoot and alone.

Dad crawled into his tent. "Go to sleep, Rachel," he said.

"I'll just sit by the fire for a bit more," I told him.

You couldn't put much over Dad. He knew what I was up to. "He won't come," he said. "He's wild and frightened. We'll call out a search party when we get back."

I sat there alone, but not alone, as the fire crackled and tossed sparks into the arms of the watching tree tops. The noises of the night kept me company.

I stared into the dark fringes of the forest. Watching for the watcher. Waiting for the waiter. Willing Philip to come.

At last the fire died and I shared the dark blanket of the night with the unseen creatures of the bush.

Quietly I walked to the edge of the trees and broke off a piece of cake. I placed it on a rock. A few metres away I did the same. I made a trail of cake leading to the edge of the dying fire.

Then I sat and waited.

Minutes passed. And hours. The moon slowly climbed behind the clouds. I struggled to keep my eyes open. But failed. You can only fight off sleep for so long. Then it wins and your head droops and your eyes close. That's what happened to me.

8

How long I dozed for I don't know. But something woke me. Not a noise. Nothing from the forest. More like a thought or a dream. Or the memory of a woman's voice. I woke with a start and stared around the clearing. Something was different. Something was missing.

The first piece of cake. It was gone.

At that moment I half saw two things. High in a tree off to one side was a shadowy figure, watching from a branch. And on the edge of the clearing was someone else. I was sure it was Philip.

It was.

He cautiously crept forward into the open. Shadows fell across his body. He was still dressed like a beggar. Hundreds of flapping rags hung from his body.

The boy's eyes darted from side to side. He looked first at the cake and then at me. He crept forward a few steps and bent and picked up the cake. The moon slid out from its hiding place.

And Philip stood there, revealed. For a moment I couldn't take it in. Couldn't make sense of what my eyes were telling me. His rags flapped in the breeze. But the night was still and there was no breeze.

They were alive. His rags seethed and crawled and squeaked.

The wild boy was covered in bats. They hung from

his arms and hair and chest. He was dressed in live bats. I couldn't believe it. Only his eyes were clear. His beautiful, dark eyes. I gave a scream and staggered backwards.

The movement alarmed Philip and he threw his arms across his face. He was like a living book with its grey pages ruffling in a storm. Two bats flew up into the air and swooped under the trees.

Philip looked at me in fear and then up at the circling bats. Without a word he held his hands up to his mouth and started to whistle softly. The bats in the trees flew straight back and attached themselves to his hair. The others became calm.

"Sorry," I said in a hoarse voice. "I didn't mean to scare you." There were lots of things I wanted to say. My stomach felt strange. I could feel myself blushing. I wanted to say something tender. Something caring. Something that would make us friends. Or more than friends. But all I could think of saying was, "Have some cake."

Philip stared at me. And then at the cake. I could see that he wasn't sure. I wondered if he had ever seen a girl before.

"I'm your friend," I said. "I won't hurt you, I promise."

He was hungry. I guess that he hadn't tasted cake

for a long, long time. Maybe he had been eating bat food. Fruit and moths and things.

He gave a sort of smile. Only a small one. But it was enough to make my heart beat so fast that it hurt. Philip took a step towards the next piece of cake. He was starting to trust me. Maybe even to like me. As quick as a snake striking he pounced on the cake and began munching.

He ate like a five year old, shoving the cake in with both hands and smearing crumbs all over his face.

If only I could get him to trust me. I might be able to talk to him. To make him stay. He swallowed the last crumb and then just stood there staring into my eyes.

Slowly I took a step forward. "It's OK," I whispered. "It's OK."

The bats murmured and fluttered. He was ready to run. But he let me approach. An invisible bond was holding us together.

"Aagh . . ." There was a terrible scream from the tree tops. A branch broke with a crack. The shadowy figure I'd seen plunged down, grabbing at branches and yelling. He landed with a thump and lay there groaning. It was Dad.

The bats scattered into the air like a swarm of huge bees. Philip's cloak was gone. He stood there,

11

naked. He glared at me. He thought we had tried to trap him. He raised his fist and then, thinking better of it, fled into the forest.

"Come back," I yelled. Tears flooded down my face. "Please come back."

But only the bats stayed, circling above me, squeaking in fright.

I ran over to Dad. "Sorry," he said. "I couldn't let you meet him alone. I had to keep an eye on you."

"Are you OK?" I asked.

Dad tried to stand but he couldn't. "Sprained ankle," he groaned.

We both looked up at the circling cloud of bats. They didn't seem to know where to go. A sound drifted on the night air. "Sh . . ." said Dad.

A soft, squeaking whistle pierced the night. It was the whistling noise Philip made through his fingers. The bats squeaked frantically, circled once and flew off after the sound. Dad and I were alone in the dark, silent clearing.

Frenzied thoughts filled my mind. Philip, Philip. We have betrayed you. Dad, how could you spy on me? Dad, are you hurt?

Dad was groaning and holding his ankle. "That's the end of the expedition," he said. "I can't walk a step."

"But what about the bats? The cave might fall on them. The whole colony will die unless we blow up the cave."

"I'm sorry, Rachel," said Dad. "I can't move. And you can't go alone. We'll stay here. The Rangers know our route. They'll send a helicopter when we don't arrive back on time. We'll be safe if we stay here."

I took a deep breath. "But that's in three days. What if the cave collapses? I'm going on my own."

"Don't be silly," said Dad. "You've never even seen a stick of dynamite. I wouldn't let you anywhere near it. You'd kill yourself." He grabbed his pack and held it tight. The dynamite was inside.

"There's something you haven't thought of," I said.

"Yes?"

"Philip. He is covered in bats. He wears them like clothes."

"So?" said Dad.

"And he whistles through his fingers and calls them."

"Yes?"

"Where do you think he lives? He is a bat boy. He must live in that cave with the bats. And the roof is about to fall in. We have to save him."

Dad didn't say anything for quite a bit. He knew I was right.

"You're not going anywhere," he said at last. "You might get lost. You can't handle dynamite. The boy won't come out of the cave anyway. He's a wild thing. He hasn't spoken to anyone since he was five. No. We wait here until help arrives. And that's the end of it."

When your father says, "That's the end of it", it usually is.

But not this time.

I don't know how to say it. But I couldn't get Philip's face out of my mind. My stomach was churning over. My face was hot. Just thinking about him gave me the shivers. That cave might fall in at any time. He could die alone, covered in bats. Far from his people. In nine years he had never felt the touch of a woman's hand.

"I'm going," I said. "And you can't stop me."

"No," Dad said with an iron face. "You're only fourteen. I forbid it."

"You've got a sprained ankle and can't move," I said. "You can't forbid anything. Goodbye." I just turned around and started walking out of the clearing into the night forest.

"All right. All right, Rachel," he called. "But come back. You have to prepare. Take food and a compass. Ropes. Everything. Otherwise there will be two dead teenagers."

So that's what happened. I packed my knapsack

with food and everything I might need. Except the dynamite. There was no way Dad would even take his hand off it.

By morning I was ready to leave. I headed off in the direction of Bat Peaks. The mountain loomed above us. Like a pair of giant wings. "Remember," yelled Dad. "Don't go inside the cave. Promise."

"Yes," I said as I pushed into the bush. "I promise."

It was tough going. The higher I went the more difficult it became. The trees gave way to giant boulders and scrub. My knees were raw and bleeding. My feet were sore.

But I didn't care. I had to get Philip and the bats out of that cave. But how?

I held my fingers up to my lips and blew. Nothing except a rush of hot air. Not so much as a squeak. If I could learn to whistle through my fingers I might be able to call him. And bring out the bats.

But I just couldn't get the hang of it. I always admired those kids at school who could whistle through their fingers.

The sun rose high above me and then began to lower itself towards the rim of the mountains. Before I knew it, the sky was growing dark.

I was perched high above the forest on a mountain ledge. The trees below looked like the surface of an ocean gently rippling in the last of the sunlight. Cockatoos circled, screeching above their roosts. I jiggled down into my sleeping bag and hoped that I wouldn't roll over the edge in my sleep.

Not that I did sleep. The ground was hard. And I couldn't stop thinking about Philip.

So I practised finger whistling. I blew until my lips were parched and dry. But not a sound could I get. It was hopeless.

The next day I scrambled up and on. Rocks tumbled and crashed under my feet. They bounded into the valley way below. I became reckless. I didn't stop to rest.

I knew that time was passing too quickly. I dreaded to think what I might find when I reached the bat cave.

I stopped for nothing. Not even to use the compass. After all, there was only one way to go. Up.

That's how I became lost. I found myself on a rocky outcrop. Tumbled into a crevasse. Lay dazed for hours. Lost my pack. Lost my compass. Lost my senses.

In the end I crawled out and sat and cried. I had no map. No way of knowing where I was. I was totally lost.

That's when I saw it. Just hanging there on a bramble. A leather pouch. I stumbled over and grabbed it. I fumbled with the catch and looked inside. The green-coloured stone with a hole in it.

Philip must have dropped it again. Twice in three days?

I couldn't believe that he would keep dropping something so precious. It was the only thing he had to remind him of his mother.

I smiled. I told myself that he left it there on purpose.

For me. To show me the way. That's what I thought anyway. That's what I hoped.

I grabbed the pouch and stumbled on. On to the very top. On to where the sheer rock cliffs fell down on every side.

A small bridge of rock spanned a drop into the valley miles below. It was so far that my head swam.

And there, on the other side, hanging under an enormous shelf was what I had come for. The bat cave.

Normally I would not have crossed that rocky bridge. Not for anything.

But somehow I forced my trembling legs over. Until I stood there peering at the cave, staring into its black jaws.

All was silent except for the soft breath of the cold mountain breeze.

I looked at the roof of the cave. It seemed OK to

me. How did Dad know that it was going to fall in?

I held my fingers to my mouth and blew. Nothing. I couldn't get a whistle. Not a squeak. It was hopeless.

"Philip," I called. "Philip, come out. The cave is going to collapse."

Silence was the only reply.

I forgot my promise to Dad. Or I pushed it into the back of my mind. I'm not sure which.

With thumping heart I made my way into the gloom. Water pinged in the distance. A soft burbling noise surrounded me.

As my eyes became used to the dark I could make out a huge boulder in the roof. It seemed to move. It did move. It was covered in thousands of hanging bats. Their wings rippled like a blanket floating on a lake.

How long before that rock would fall? I trembled. "Philip," I called urgently. "Philip."

No answer. I raised my voice. "Come out, you stupid boy," I shouted. "Come out."

It was not Philip who was stupid. It was me. My voice echoed terribly around the walls. It bounced off the rocks. It shook the dry air.

Without a speck of warning the living boulder above plunged to the ground. It shook the mountain to its roots. It filled the cave with choking dust.

My voice had dislodged the boulder.

Thousands of bats mingled with the dust. Circling, screaming. Screeching. I turned and fled into the glaring sunlight. Another boulder fell. The sound of its smash pummelled the walls. More rocks fell.

"Philip," I screamed. "Philip, come out."

Dust, like smoke from a fallen chimney, billowed into the mountain air. And through it came Philip. Blood flowed from a deep wound in his head. He staggered out and fell at my feet. Unconscious.

I dragged him clear of the mouth of the cave. I pulled him towards the rocky bridge. And then stopped and stared, filled with terror at the sight.

The bridge had broken. Fallen into the valley below. We were trapped on the mountain top. There was no way back.

Naked. Not a stitch on.

Poor Philip. Lying there on the bare mountain. Exposed to the wind. Was he dead? I didn't know.

I should have put my jumper over him. Covered his nakedness. But there wasn't time. Rocks were still falling. There was no way down. And the bats. The bats were doomed. "Help. Someone help."

No one answered. I was alone.

I held my fists up to my mouth and blew. I wanted so badly to save the bats. I tried to whistle loudly but nothing came.

The bats were still in there. They would die because of me. Because I raised my voice and dis-turbed the rocks. And Philip. Would he die too?

He opened his eyes. He looked at me. Was he accusing me? Did his eyes say that I had murdered his friends?

No, they did not. He smiled. He tried to speak but he couldn't. Instead he touched the pouch that hung around my neck. His mother's stone.

"This," I said. He nodded and once more closed his eyes.

I took out the green stone and stared at it. I knew what to do. I began to blow through the hole.

The air was filled with a whistle. A strong, clear, squeaking. The most beautiful sound I had ever heard.

The cave echoed thunder. Not of falling rocks but of beating wings. Hundreds, thousands, millions of wings. The bats surged out of the cave. They dark-ened the sky. They filled the mountain top until nothing could be seen but a swirling swarm of grey. I had saved the colony.

Philip opened his eyes and smiled. He took the stone from my fingers and blew. He whistled his own message to the bats.

They dropped out of the sky like autumn leaves in a storm. I shrieked. They grabbed my hair. My feet. They pierced my jumper with tiny claws. The bats hung from me like rags.

I stared at Philip. He was no longer naked, but like me wore a living cloak. Bat boy. Bat girl. Stranded. Together on Bat Peaks.

The bats beat their wings in a terrible rhythm. They stirred up a storm of squealing fury.

My feet left the ground. I was flying. Carried up, up, up. Lifted into the sky by a flurry of flapping wings. Held by tiny feet.

The mountain lay far beneath. I saw an explosion of dust spurt out from the cave below. The roof had caved in.

I gasped in shock at the sight of the valleys below. Like the prey of a mountain eagle I was lifted between the mountain tops.

And above me, Philip, carried by his coat of friends, soared and swooped in the empty sky.

He waved and pointed.

Far, far beneath, in the tangled mat of trees was a wisp of smoke. Dad's camp fire.

The bats began to descend. Taking us down through the biting air.

For the first time Philip spoke. He pointed down at the campfire and said just one word.

"Home."

And that is where we went.

Fixer

Anthony Masters

Jack rolled over on the muddy ground in the goal mouth, hugging the ball tight as Clapham United's fans roared their applause.

"Brilliant save!" yelled Rob as Jack struggled to his feet. He'd done it again. How long was his luck going to last?

But surely it wasn't luck, was it? It was skill. Ted Gill, United's coach, had told him that over and over again.

"Remember you've got talent. Luck isn't in it." Ted had been almost impatient, for Jack never thought much of himself. Now Ted was cheering hard.

But Jack's elation died away as Barney Dexter's big, confident smile swam into his mind. "You'll fix next Saturday's final, Jack. You'll let Albion in."

Today was a friendly. It didn't matter to Barney. But next week did. If Jack couldn't fix the match against Wimbledon Albion, Barney would fix *him*.

And then what would Mum think when she found out he'd been shoplifting?

"What's the matter?" asked Rob as they ran to the changing rooms after the match. "You look like you've let 'em all in, not kept 'em all out."

"I'm knackered," was all Jack could say, and Rob stared after him in surprise as he grabbed his bike and began the long ride home.

Jack didn't want to hurt his mother. She had been hurt already – hurt so badly by the drunken driver that she had been in a wheelchair ever since. The man had driven off, leaving her unconscious, but the police had eventually tracked him down. He had got off with a heavy fine and two years' ban. That wasn't enough for Jack. He would like to have killed him.

So much had gone wrong for his mother. Dad had walked out long ago, and had never contacted either of them again. Then there had been the accident that had left her paralysed.

Now Jack was going to give her a final blow.

As he cycled down the hill he remembered the amazing news that Ted Gill had given him a few weeks ago.

"You're going to be picked for the training scheme. I reckon you should be proud of yourself, Jack. Of course there's the coaching fees and the travel expenses . . ." Ted had looked at him anxiously.

"What with your mum and all . . ." He had paused, wondering how to go on. "Will you have any problem about the money?"

You bet I will, Jack had thought. Even with all Mum's allowances we're always flat broke. But aloud he'd said, "I'll manage."

Jack knew that Mum wouldn't be able to afford the fees. He already had an early morning paper round and had tried to get the evening one, but had lost out to Tim Hawkins. So Jack had decided to start shoplifting, reckoning that if he managed to steal food, Mum would have enough money left to pay for his football training.

Jack wasn't dishonest by nature. In fact, he had never even contemplated doing such a terrible thing in his life. But there seemed no alternative.

"I've got the evening newspaper round," he had lied to his mother when he got home. "I can get some of the shopping with that if you can afford to pay my coaching fees out of your allowance."

His mother, delighted and proud, had only one worry. "You'll be exhausted. Two newspaper rounds – and then all that shopping."

But Jack had told her the cycling would keep him fit, and eventually she had been satisfied.

He had hated lying to her and he had hated shoplifting. But once Jack had stolen a pot of jam and a couple of tins of baked beans, the conscience that usually gave him a hard time seemed to get buried deep inside.

Jack took a shoulder bag to the supermarket, putting a few stolen items inside whilst the rest that he was actually going to pay for went straight into the trolley. It was too easy. What's more, he was well-known at the supermarket. After all, he'd been shopping here for the last two years and most of the checkout staff knew about his mother's accident. No one suspected him. Everyone thought he was a hero.

Jack had even begun to salve his conscience by convincing himself that he had every right to steal.

The supermarket was a huge chain. They would never miss a few stolen goods. Mum was paralysed. They had no money. It was all he could do. There was no alternative.

"I can afford your training money," Mum had reassured Jack as they had their tea. "So when do you start?"

"After the final. The final we're going to win. We'll take Albion. No bother."

Later, he had helped her out of her wheelchair and into bed as he did every night. Mum had got so thin that she was very easy to lift. He'd do the same in the morning. It always terrified him.

"Got you!' Barney Dexter had been holding a small camera.

Jack had gazed at him in horror. He'd forgotten that Barney was a shelf-filler in the evenings. A year older than Jack, he was one of the school's worst bullies.

"What are you talking about?"

"I saw you putting stuff in that bag last night so I decided to bring in the camera my granny gave me for Christmas." His grin had widened. "It's a Polaroid. Look at you then."

He had held up the print, which showed Jack furtively snatching a tin of grapefruit segments from the shelf.

"So what?" Desperately he had tried to brazen it out.

"Where is it then? I don't see the tin in your trolley."

"I must have made a mistake," Jack had spluttered, his face reddening, the sweat standing out on his forehead, his heart hammering so much that it hurt.

"It's in your bag."

"Keep your voice down."

"Only if you show me."

Jack had paused, panic blinding him, not knowing what to do.

Of course the tin was in his shoulder bag and so were several others, as well as half a pound of sausages.

"All right," he had muttered, fighting back the desperate tears, trying to keep control. "What are you going to do?"

"It's more like what *you're* going to do, Jack."

Barney had begun to replenish the stocks of canned fruit while Jack stood miserably beside him.

"You know my brother Warren?"

Jack had nodded. Warren was in his year. He was also the star striker for Wimbledon Albion, the team Clapham needed to beat at the final on Saturday. A dreadful flicker of understanding had raced across Jack's mind.

Barney had looked up, his grin malicious. "I can see you're beginning to get the message."

Jack had been determined he wasn't. "I don't get you."

"Try harder. You're going to let Warren in, aren't you?"

"He won't get near me."

"Yes, he will. And you're going to let him in. Albion are going to win!"

"They're not!"

"Because you're going to fix the match. And if you don't, I'll take these prints to the manager here."

"That doesn't prove a thing."

"Didn't you hear what I said, thicko? I said – prints. In the plural, right?" Barney had reached into the pocket of his overall and held the second instant photograph close to Jack's eyes. This one all too clearly showed him putting a can of beans into his black shoulder bag.

"Get me?"

"Got you," Jack had said, feeling sick.

"Of course, if you let Warren in I won't show them to anyone."

Jack had tried to make a grab for the print, but Barney had been too quick for him, shoving it back into his pocket.

Without thinking of the consequences Jack had bunched his fists.

"Don't start anything," Barney had said quietly. "If you do, you'll give yourself away."

Jack had walked home, his bag of stolen goods over his shoulder and the ones he hadn't stolen in two large plastic bags. What was he going to do? he wondered. Barney Dexter had him completely in his power. If he was nicked for shoplifting what would Mum say? What would it do to her?

"Everything comes in threes," she had once said bitterly. Jack had reminded her that it hadn't.

"Not yet," she had replied gloomily.

Dad walking out. The drunk driver. And now her only son on a shoplifting charge. Who said everything didn't come in threes?

With two days to go to the match, Jack found that he couldn't sleep and was becoming increasingly irritable. He even took it out on Mum.

"It's the big one on Saturday," she said enthusiastically over breakfast. "Aren't you nervous?"

"Not really." Jack's voice was flat as he pushed his cornflakes round his plate.

"You seem to have lost your appetite."

No wonder, he thought. He was eating cornflakes from one of the miniature packets he'd nicked. He could hardly get them down without choking.

"I may be able to get to watch the match for once. Mrs Jennings said she'd bring me down."

"I wouldn't bother."

"Don't you want me there?" She was instantly hurt.

Jack stood up, knowing how badly he was upsetting her, yet knowing how much more deeply upset she would be if he was found out. He'd *have* to let the shots in. He'd *have* to fix the match. He didn't have any choice. But suppose Barney Dexter didn't destroy those prints? Suppose he went on blackmailing him for ever?

"I've got to get to school."

"But you're early."

"Bye, Mum." He gave her a peck on the cheek and was gone.

Looking back, Jack saw his mother gazing after him like a wounded animal.

Barney was waiting for him by the lockers.

"You're going to fix the match, aren't you?" A dark red mist seemed to have drifted into Jack's eyes, and inside he felt tight as a drum – as if he could hardly breathe. "Please," he whispered. "I *can't*."

"Your mum's not going to like you being done for shoplifting, is she?" Barney grinned. "Not after all she's been through."

31

The red mist darkened until it was so dense that Jack could hardly see. "You leave her out of it."

"The police won't."

Barney was taller than Jack and much stronger. Nevertheless, Jack threw himself at him, punching and kicking, yelling abuse.

As the blows connected, Barney was forced back against the lockers, head down, protecting his face with his hands, too afraid to fight back, as an interested crowd began to collect.

Then Rob arrived, broke through the spectators and grabbed Jack round the waist, pulling him away from Barney, trying to defuse the violence. Jack struggled in his grasp.

Then the bell went and the crowd immediately dispersed.

"I'll get you for that," Barney muttered as he limped away. "You see if I don't."

But Jack knew he already had.

"What on earth was that all about?" Rob asked.

"He said something about my mum."

"What?"

"It doesn't matter."

"You know what he's like."

"You bet I do."

"You don't want to start getting into fights. Not with the match a couple of days away."

"Get off my back!" yelled Jack, all his frustrated rage and anxiety returning.

"I'm only trying to help." Rob looked like Mum. Hurt and bewildered.

"Don't bother." Jack ran off in the direction of his tutor group.

Jack stood in the goal mouth, poised and ready. The last couple of nights had been really bad and he had hardly slept at all for worrying about what he was going to have to do. He hadn't been near the super-market, getting what they needed from the more expensive corner shop, and Mum had been surprised at how quickly her allowance had been used up again.

"I thought things would be easier with that extra money from your evening newspaper round, but it doesn't seem to be making as much difference as I thought," she had said last night, totting up her petty cash book.

Immediately Jack's lies had got more complicated. "I've lost the round, Mum. I couldn't face telling you."

"But how?" She had been bewildered again. "Mr Dawson's always thought so highly of you."

"I was a bit late the other night and he was in a bad mood. So he took the round off me and gave it to Will Rogers."

"That's not fair."

"It doesn't matter."

"Anyway," she had said. "I'm glad."

"Glad?" Now it had been Jack's turn to be bewildered.

"It was too much for you. Draining all your energy. It could even have wrecked the match."

The match was wrecked already, thought Jack as Warren Dexter came pounding towards him.

"What's the matter, Jack?" Ted Gill was furious with him at half-time. So were the rest of the team as they gathered together for a briefing. But the briefing was more like an inquest.

Only Rob looked concerned. Everybody else was out for his blood.

"You've got to wake up!" snapped Ted Gill. "You let two easy ones through. Why?"

"I don't know."

"You looked like a performing seal," commented Dean Harrison.

"More like a ballet dancer," added Jake Thompson nastily.

"Who asked for *your* views?" Ted Gill turned on them angrily. "We all have our off days. Jack's having one of his. But we're going to save the match, lads, and I'll tell you how."

As Ted Gill talked tactics, Jack felt relieved that his mother hadn't turned up to watch him blow the game away. Not so far, anyway.

Ted had been right. The shots had been too easy to let through. Far too easy. What was he going to do?

Everyone would soon realize he was fixing the match. If anyone was having an off day, it had to be Warren Dexter.

"Your mum's here," said Rob as they walked back to the pitch.

Sure enough, she was on the sideline in her wheelchair, barely able to stop giving Jack a wave. Her appearance was the final blow.

Mrs Jennings was hovering behind his mother.

Maybe she'd been late or her car had packed up.

"Show your mum what you can do," said Rob. "Don't let her down."

Something clicked in Jack's mind. Of course he couldn't let Mum down. Not now. Not on the field. She was going to be properly let down later, he told himself. Even if he let the shots through he'd never get Barney off his back. He knew that now. How was she going to like having a thief for a son?

He glanced towards the sideline. Barney Dexter had been standing there all the way through the first half, a smile fixed on his big meaty face.

Now Jack was going to blow that stupid grin away.

Warren Dexter was on him again, running towards the goal mouth, manoeuvring the muddy ball with rather more skill while the Albion supporters went mad, cheering and shouting, chanting his name.

Jack gazed at him intently, trying to read his mind, watching his feet. Where was he going to put the ball?

Had his coach given him a talking-to? He seemed much more on form. For a moment Jack thought he knew what Warren's tactics were going to be. Then, just in time, he realized he was trying to fool him.

Jack dived as the ball shot towards the net.

It was the turn of the Clapham United supporters

to go wild as Jack made his save, scrambled to his feet and kicked the ball out of the penalty area.

"Well saved, Jack!" shouted Ted Gill. He was standing next to Barney Dexter, whose grin was still firmly in place.

Jack knew that Barney thought the save was just part of his fixing strategy. Let in two, keep one out, let in the others, so they would look like mistakes. But now Barney had another think coming.

Jack turned to glance at his mother, who was clapping delightedly and shouting his name.

His love for her welled up inside him with such intensity that he could feel tears pricking at the backs of his eyes.

What was the best of the two options? Let her see him fail as United's goalie? Or see him branded as a thief?

Jack saved two more shots in spectacular style. His sudden return to form made Clapham United attack much more aggressively and soon there were two balls in Albion's net and it looked as if the game might end in a draw.

Then, just before the referee blew the whistle for full-time, Rob scored.

As the Clapham supporters cheered for all they were worth, Jack turned to face Barney Dexter. He was in exactly the same position on the sideline, the grin still on his face. But he was holding up a couple of prints and Jack knew exactly what they were, and what he was going to do with them.

Then he had a sudden and very risky idea. "You did well, Jack. You really did well." His mother looked younger, full of life – exhausted but also enormously excited. He had not seen her this way for a long, long time.

Her praise was worth more than Ted Gill's, more than his team-mates', more than Rob's.

But Jack realized that if his plan didn't work out – and it was a long shot – then his mother might be badly hurt once too often.

"I'll be home soon, Mum. I'm just going to . . ." he hesitated, "cycle back with Rob. We want to talk over the game."

"I bet you do, love," she said. "But don't be too self-critical. You were wonderful."

Wonderful? he thought. I'm not wonderful. I'm a thief.

Jack found Rob in the changing room.

"I want to talk to you."

"What about?" Rob looked at Jack curiously.

"My sudden return to form."

"Warren seemed to have the same problem in the first half. But what went wrong with you?"

Slowly, hesitantly, Jack began to tell him. When

he had finished, there was a long silence.

"Come on then,' said Jack. 'Say you despise me."

"I don't."

"You should."

"You were set up and you fought back. Now you've got me to help you."

"We want to see the manager." Rob was insistent.

"What about?" The supervisor looked put out.

"It's important."

"Can't I help?"

"Not really." Jack was trembling.

"Very well. Step this way – but I hope you're not going to waste Mr Johnson's time."

"No," said Rob. "We're not going to waste a second of it."

The office was small and functional with a few chairs, a couple of filing cabinets, a telephone and a nameplate on the desk: *Graham Johnson*.

The manager was young and friendly, unlike the supervisor, who snapped the door shut dis-approvingly.

"Do sit down," he told the boys.

They did as he said. A long silence developed. Jack's mouth was so dry that he could hardly bring the words out. Then he forced himself.

"I – I took some stuff," he stuttered. "Because my

mum's ill. We don't have enough money. I've been picked for the football training scheme. I can't afford the fees. She's in a wheelchair. Mum can't afford the fees either. I told her I had a round. A newspaper round. But I didn't. I never had one – at least, I did in the mornings, but not in the evenings." Jack came to a shuddering halt, knowing that he wasn't making any sense.

He glanced at Rob but he was looking away, red in the face with embarrassment.

Jack plunged on.

"Barney Dexter – he took these photographs. Like of me nicking stuff. He said if I didn't fix the match, he'd take them to you."

As if on cue, there was a knock at the door and the supervisor reappeared, looking even more irritated.

"Yes. What is it now?" asked Graham Johnson briskly.

"There's someone else to see you."

"Who is it?"

"Guy called Dexter. Works for us part-time as a shelf-filler. Says he's got something you should see."

"Tell him I'm busy right now." The supervisor closed the door reluctantly.

"Now look," said Graham Johnson. "Why don't we begin all over again? I didn't really understand what you were on about."

40

This time Jack spoke more slowly and clearly. But as he told his story, he could already imagine telling it again to a policeman.

When he had finished, all Graham Johnson could say was, "I see." The silence filled the room like cold lead. Then he spoke again. "I think you've been punished enough, don't you?"

Jack gazed at him, unable to believe his ears.

"Our usual policy is to prosecute shoplifters, but I'm not going to this time. In fact, I'm going to ask you if you'd like a job. There's a vacancy going."

"Is there?" Waves of shock filled him, and Jack could hardly grasp what was being said. Rob was looking incredulous.

"It's just come up. A shelf-filler."

"But I'd be working with—"

"Dexter's leaving."

"Is he?"

Graham Johnson got to his feet. "So how did the match go then?" he asked.

As Rob and Jack left the manager's office, feeling not only bewildered but amazingly relieved, they saw Barney Dexter standing outside, the prints clasped in his hand, his grin unusually strained.

"Mr Dexter?" Graham Johnson's voice was cold. "Would you like to come in?"

"Thanks for coming with me, Rob," said Jack as they walked over to their bikes.

"That's all right."

"I can hardly believe what's happened."

"Neither can I. But what are you going to tell your mum?"

"The truth."

"Is that a good idea?"

"If I don't, Barney might get to her first. If I can tell you and the manager, I can tell Mum."

"Want me to come?"

"Not this time."

Rob nodded, and Jack knew that he understood.

When Jack got back home, Mum was in the kitchen, doing all she could to make tea on her own. She was still full of excitement.

"You were great, Jack," she said.

"I wasn't till you turned up."

"I'm sorry. Mrs Jennings' car broke down and—"

"You saved me. And then I stopped the shots. But I've got something to tell you – something I'm ashamed of."

She looked up at him calmly. "What is it, Jack?"

Slowly, and then more confidently, he began to tell his mother what had happened.

A Gap in the Dark

Helen Dunmore

"Com-ing!"

"She never counts up to twenty!" hissed Matthew as we skidded across the polished hall. No one was around to stop us, so up the stairs we went, three at a time, never mind the noise.

Anne was slow. She'd still be in the kitchen asking Eliza, "Did you see them? Which way did they go? You've *got* to tell me!"

We raced along the gallery, and nearly cannoned into Mistress Bowman, who was carrying a heap of linen from one of the bedrooms. I slowed down and curtsied politely, but she frowned and said, "Not so fast, Judith. Matthew, surely you should be at your studies." She looked at me coldly. Perhaps she thought I was stopping Matthew from working at his Latin? No, it was more than that. She'd changed. She never smiled at me any more, or asked after my parents. Perhaps she didn't like me coming to the

43

Hall? But I hadn't got time to think about that.

"In here," said Matthew, and pushed me into a small bare room. I'd never been there before. It was square, with panelled walls, and there was no furniture but a little white bed in the corner, and a candlestick on the floor beside it. The room was right at the end of the passage, and if Anne came we weren't going to get away. I looked out of the window but it was much too high for us to climb down over the roof. And there was Anne again.

"I'm com-ing. I know where you are!"

She didn't, of course. She always said that. She was still down in the hall, from the sound of it. But what was Matthew doing, feeling along the panels, pressing, stopping, pressing again? His hands looked like Blind Thomas's when he tapped his way through our village. A dark gap appeared where the wall had been. A hole. What was it?

Matthew shoved me forward.

"Quick! Get in!"

I stepped over the threshold and into the hole. I couldn't see much and I held my hands out, feeling for the wall. There was nothing but cool, empty, black space. Matthew bent down and pulled something. Very smoothly and quickly the door slid shut. Black, velvety darkness covered me like a mask. I raised my hands to my face as if to pull it off. I

couldn't see my fingers. I couldn't see anything. I took a step back but the floor seemed to swing under me and I was afraid I'd fall.

Matthew whispered, "There. She'll never find us now."

He was so near, I could feel his warmth. It wasn't so bad with both of us there, close together, but I'd have hated to be shut in there on my own. The darkness was stifling – not like night-dark or any dark I've ever known. I strained my eyes and red blobs floated in front of them.

"Where are we?" I whispered.

"Ssh, she's coming."

We heard Anne. First of all, the door banged open

45

and there was a triumphant shout of "Got you!" which tailed off into, "Judith? Matthew? I know you're in here. You're only teasing me. I shall tell Mother." She moved round the room. She must have been just the other side of the panelling, so close we could have touched her but for the wood in our way. Everything went silent, but I felt she was still there, perhaps listening for us. Then, very slowly and disappointedly, her feet went away.

"She's gone."

"I wish we had a candle."

"There's nothing much to see. Just a cell, then the passage goes right back."

"How strange. You wouldn't expect to find anything like this in a new building."

Bowman Hall had been built fifteen years ago, by Matthew's father. It was the finest house for miles around.

"My father had the hole put in," said Matthew. "It was done on purpose."

"Why?"

"In case anyone ever needed to hide. No one knows about it. Only my mother and father, and me, and you. And perhaps Eliza does."

"And the builders."

"No. Only one man worked on the hole. My father trusted him."

I didn't like talking without being able to see Matthew's face. We found ourselves whispering, even though we knew Anne had gone. The darkness pressed down on me, making me feel tired.

"Let's go out. I'm sure she's gone." Matthew moved and I heard a tiny click, the sort a well-oiled lock makes. Then a slice of white appeared, like a slice of cake. It hurt my eyes. We stumbled out of the hole, blinking, and Matthew quickly closed up the panel again. You couldn't see a trace of the door once it was shut, no matter how closely you looked. Then we heard Mistress Bowman's voice calling, "Matthew! Matthew!"

She sounded angry. Anne must have said we'd tricked her and run away. We often did. It was Anne who wanted to play hide-and-seek, not us.

"I must go home," I said quickly, before anyone else could suggest it.

"Judith. You won't tell anyone about it, will you? It's very important."

"Course I won't. I've never told on you, have I?" I saw suddenly how important it was to Matthew. He looked older, and serious.

"Listen," I said, "I'm your friend. Of course I'll keep it secret."

"Because one day . . . we might need to use it."

*

That was the last time I was asked to visit Matthew at the Hall. After that everything changed. We had to meet down by the river, or in the woods, where no one saw us. My mother kept me busy milking and churning with my sister Becky. When I said I wanted to see Matthew, she frowned, the way Mistress Bowman had done.

"You're to keep away from the Bowmans now, Judith. These are dangerous times for friendships between them and us. Don't you know they follow the old religion? You know what that means?"

I nodded. I did know. I'd heard it all round the village. Papists were dangerous. They wanted to kill our Queen and bring the King of Spain here to rule over us. There were plots everywhere. We'd have good men burnt alive at Smithfield again, the way it was under Bloody Mary. Ours was a good Protestant village, loyal to the Queen. That was what they said, but I knew it couldn't all be true. After all, Matthew was my friend. And I noticed that my mother and father never joined in when such things were said. I looked at my mother. Her face was anxious. Afraid. Afraid for me, the way she used to be when I played too near the fire when I was little.

"You must tell Matthew you have work to do at home. It's true enough."

"The Bowmans are our neighbours, Susannah," said my father.

"Don't let anyone hear you talking like that, John. Don't you know that there are Government spies everywhere, even in our village?"

A look passed between my parents.

A look I couldn't understand. There was a secret, and I was shut out of it.

Suddenly it seemed as if everyone in our village was whispering about the Bowmans. People said a woman had been executed in York for hiding a Papist priest. Margaret something, her name was. Everyone was afraid. It's hard to describe what it was like. The whispering was like a shadow which covered everything and got in everywhere. What if the Bowmans were plotting? What if they were hiding priests? Would they bring down the Government spies and torturers on us all? My mother listened, but I noticed that she never said a word. She didn't smile any more, either, and there was a new line on her forehead, between her eyes.

I was taking a basket of eggs down the village street when I first saw the man. He was on a fine mare, but she was worn out and sweating, with a white lather on her flanks. He was a gallant in a feathered hat and a velvet cloak, but he was covered in dust and dirt as if he'd come a long way, riding hard. He slowed the mare beside me and I could smell the heat of her. She was trembling and her flanks were going in and out, quickly. I knew she could not go on more than a mile.

"Is there a tavern here where I can rest myself and the mare?" he called.

"Joe Barraclough will serve you, sir. You'll find him outside the tavern."

Joe was always outside the tavern, lounging and drinking ale in the sun while his wife cooked and served and wiped and cleaned. Still, he'd feed and groom the mare. He was good with horses.

"Thank you," said the man. He smiled at me, and I noticed how warm his smile was – not at all like the gallants in York who'd as soon ride their horses' hooves over your feet as slow down for you. Then, suddenly, his smile froze. He stared at me. His eyes widened, almost as if he recognized me – as if he was about to say my name.

"Who are you?" he asked, in a small dry voice. His throat must have been full of dust.

"My name is Judith, sir. Judith Hestone."

He let his breath out in a sigh. "Ah. Hestone. Of course." His hands were tight on the reins. The mare shivered, then put her head down and nuzzled my hand. I was burning with questions. Why *"of course"*? Why did he seem to know me?

"Joe Barraclough's tavern," he said, as if remembering something a long way back. "I must go there now. Goodbye, Judith," and he walked the mare on, leaving me looking after him.

It was not so long after that I saw a knot of people coming up to our door. That wasn't unusual. People often came to talk to Father about disputes and troubles, because he could usually calm them down and find an answer. I loitered round to listen.

"You know that fine gallant in the tavern . . ."

"I swear he's not what he seems . . ."

"Joe found a box in his saddle-bag . . ."

"Evil doings – he's got a prayer book with him full of Papish prayers . . ."

"And look at his face. And the way he limps. He's no gallant. He's a priest for sure, dressed up to fox us . . ."

"And where's he going, I should like to know?"

"Bowmans! Bowman Hall for sure!"

"Bowmans!"

They all took it up, their faces red and glistening. Father couldn't calm them this time. My mother stood beside him, her face white and frantic, arguing against the people. They wouldn't listen to her, either. I'd never seen her like that before. First they wanted to seize the man at once, and tie him in Joe Barraclough's stable till the Queen's men could get here. Then another said we ought to pretend nothing was amiss and let him go on up to Bowman Hall. We'd ride for the Queen's soldiers and they'd catch him up there and catch the Bowmans too, for sheltering a Papist priest. We'll do this, they said. No, we'll do that. I stood there, feeling cold, looking at faces. There was Simon Tolliver, who rented two fields from the Bowmans. He always said the rent was too high.

"We'll lead the soldiers to Bowmans!" he shouted.

We. I was in the crowd, part of it. But was I? Matthew was my friend, more than anyone else in the village. Matthew trusted me.

"Did I ever tell on you?" I'd said. I'd told him I could keep a secret. I was his friend. I didn't have to do anything to betray Matthew. All I had to do was do nothing and stand there, part of the crowd. My friend. Matthew. I saw his face in front of me, the way it was once, white and sick because he'd hit a trout's head on a stone to kill it and it wouldn't stop flapping. I'd taken the slippery thing from him and struck it on the stone again. I never minded things like that.

I slipped back slowly out of the crowd so no one would see me go. My heart was banging. They would capture the Bowmans, Matthew and Anne and all his family. And what would they do to them? I'd heard of people being questioned, put on the rack to make them talk. Better not think about it. I went round the back of our house, keeping close to the hedge, then through the gate into the pastures. This way I could go across country to Bowman Hall. It wasn't more than a mile from the village, and I could run. I could run Becky to a standstill any day, and even Matthew couldn't beat me. They would let the priest go off on horseback, round by the lane, thinking that no one suspected him. I would cut across and be able to warn him before he reached the house. How long would it take to fetch the Queen's men? Not long. There were soldiers quartered at Riddal.

I'm a good runner, but every breath burnt and my legs were shaking as I reached the top of the lane and flopped down on the verge. I couldn't hear anything. Had he passed already? No. There it was, the faint picking noise of hooves. In a few minutes he came round the corner of the lane, going slower than ever. He was urging the mare on.

"Come on, good girl, Bess . . ."

I stood up slowly so as not to frighten the mare or the man. He knew me, and stopped, looking surprised.

"You're wandering far from home, Judith."

It might have been because I'd been running, but I couldn't speak properly. I panted.

"They're getting the Queen's men. They know who

you are. I came to warn you."

His eyes went wide and still. The mare trembled all over as if she felt something.

"How long will it take till they get here?"

"I don't know. Not more than an hour. They've only to go to Riddal, and they've taken horses."

"I'll have to leave the mare. Go across country." He was thinking aloud.

"No!" I said. "You'll be caught. You can't hide in those clothes."

Then I remembered the hole, and what Matthew had said.

"One day we might need to use it."

One day was now. I mustn't tell the priest about it yet, in case we were caught before we got to the Hall. He might give away the Bowmans' secret, if they tortured him. People did.

"There's a place. A hiding-place up at the Hall."

Then he asked me a question I didn't understand then. "Did your mother send you?"

"No, she doesn't know anything about it. Quick, we've got to hurry!"

"I'll leave the mare here," he said. "Better if they think I've taken to the woods. Poor old girl, poor Bess, will you fend for yourself?"

"She's a fine mare. Someone'll take her, and be glad to do it," I said.

He slid off the saddle and stood wearily in the lane. I could see how stiff his legs were. The mare put her head down and began to graze. He undid his saddle-bag and slung it on his back. It looked strange on top of his rich cloak. He walked so slowly, limping.

"Quick!" I said. "Men from the village will come up to guard the lanes while others fetch the soldiers."

He hobbled along, not at all like a fine gentleman.

"Can't you go faster?" I begged.

He laughed quietly, as if it didn't matter at all.

"I had a taste of the rack once," he said. "They let me go that time, but it's left a mark on my bones."

And yet he was still going round the country, dodging and hiding, even though he knew what would happen if they caught him.

"You could take my arm," I said.

We went as fast as we could, him hobbling and leaning on me. My shoulder ached from his weight. If only he'd left the saddle-bag we'd have got on better, but when I suggested he hide it in a ditch, he gasped.

"No. That's why I'm here." I knew then that he must have his priestly things in the bag, and I didn't complain about it any more.

The Hall was very quiet. We came in the back way, through the stableyard, with the doves bubbling and cooing, and Matthew's mare, Star, looking over her stable-door at us. I pushed open the kitchen door and there was Eliza. She was stirring milk over the fire, and she turned and saw us.

"What's this, Judith? You know you're not supposed to come here—"

"Quick. He's a priest. The Queen's men are coming. The men from the village are fetching them. They want to trap the Bowmans."

"God have mercy on us, and Mistress Bowman's sick with an ague. I was making this posset for her. And the master's away." Eliza held out the mixture of milk and honey as if it would solve everything.

"Where's Matthew?" I said. At least he'd help me do something. Then Eliza changed. Her big body became purposeful. Calling for Matthew, she steered us through the kitchen. A door upstairs opened and I heard Matthew clattering down.

"Where's Anne?" I asked. "She mustn't see us."

"Now where's Miss Anne? Ah, she's in the orchard, picking up eggs. The hens are laying astray again."

Possets, hens, eggs. Was that all Eliza could think of?

"Matthew!"

It didn't take more than a minute to explain to Matthew. It was strange. It seemed as if he was prepared for this. Almost as if he'd been waiting for it.

"He was going to go off cross-country but I brought him here because of the secret place," I said, and Matthew nodded. His freckles stood out, the way they did when he was angry. He bowed to the priest.

"Father," he said, "you are very welcome here. We'll have to get him upstairs, Judith."

Together, we helped the priest up the stairs. He could have managed it, only we had to hurry. At the top I looked back and saw the dusty treads we'd left across Eliza's polished floor.

"Eliza! Wipe off all the marks. They'll see where we've gone."

We looked out of the low passage window, where the window-seat was. Matthew and I used to sit there on rainy days, telling stories and eating Eliza's honey-cakes. There was the orchard. There was Anne in her blue dress, bending down and searching the long grass for eggs. And there, beyond Anne . . . Two heads. At the orchard wall. They bobbed, then looked up and over. We sank out of sight, but I'd recognized them.

"Sammy Orr and Ben Striddle."

"What about Anne? They'll frighten her."

"She doesn't know anything and anyone can tell that she doesn't. You can't call her in now."

We were in the little square room again. It was hot with the sun pouring into it. The priest let go of our shoulders and straightened himself. Matthew was already feeling the panels, trying to find the catch. His hands were clumsy but at last the panel slid and darkness appeared. The priest raised his hand. I didn't know what he was doing at first, then he made the sign of the cross. He was blessing us.

"Food!" I said. "Have we got time?"

"They're watching the house. And Anne might come in and see me carrying it up. We haven't got time."

No food or drink then. Just darkness. The priest stepped carefully over the threshold.

"Pass me my bag," he said. "Gently . . . What's in that bag is more important than I am."

"Matthew," I said, "I'll have to go in with him."

He frowned. I could almost see his thinking pass over his face.

"But it might be days, Judith. When the Queen's men get here they'll search the house but they won't leave straight away. If they suspect there's a priest-hole they'll camp here and try to starve him out."

"I can't leave now. They'll see me. They'll know I've come from the village to warn you. They know I'm your friend. They might burn the house down . . ."

It had been done to other houses. We both knew it.

"I'll bring you food. I swear it. Three scratches on the door and it'll be me. There's water in a pitcher just inside the panel, on your left."

"But why? I mean, how did you know?"

"It's always there. Just in case . . ."

Just in case. We looked at each other, then I stepped forward and the panel slid shut behind me. Darkness moved all over me like velvet, like something alive. I could hear the priest's breathing, harsh and laboured, close to me.

"Move back," I said. "The passage goes back." We edged back, back, back, until we struck cold stone wall. There was a dank smell, as if the air had been here for a long time, never changing or blowing away. It made me shiver. He must have felt it because he said in the same murmur which you couldn't have heard more than three feet away, "Don't be afraid."

Don't be afraid! He was the one who ought to be afraid. Or perhaps I was too. After all, I was hiding a priest. Betraying the people of my own village. Helping a priest to safety. That's what they'd say.

"How could you do it, Judith?"

Bloody Mary. Bonfires at Smithfield. Bringing back the Papists. The King of Spain ruling over England. But it wasn't like that. Matthew was a Papist, and I was a Protestant, but we were friends. That felt more important than anything. And I could tell from his breathing that the priest was in pain. And what would they have done to him if they'd caught him?

*

59

We waited. My breathing was jerky and my heart banged until I couldn't tell if I was hearing footsteps or not. Then, at last, we felt them. The crash of heavy boots vibrating through the house, shaking the floor, coming closer and closer. I'd never heard footsteps like those in any house before; footsteps which didn't care what noise they made, what damage they did. The air seemed to shake with them. Thick, dark, shaking air pressed against my face, filling my ears and my eyes and my mouth. Voices shouted – loud outdoor voices – angry, echoing from room to room. They didn't belong in this house. Then a crash, and a cry, and another crash as if something had been flung against the panelling. Or someone. They were in the room, just the other side of the wooden wall. I was shaking – or was it the priest shaking? Was it my hand slippery with sweat, or his? I didn't care. It didn't matter.

Then the batter of noise stopped. Everything was quiet as the inside of a grave. I knew they were listening. Listening for us. Waiting for us to give ourselves away by a cough or a whisper. Then more shouting, more footsteps, but going away from us now. I followed them in my mind – across the room, through the door, down the polished gallery.

A murmur in my ear. The priest.

"Don't stir. It's a trick. To make us think they have gone."

I couldn't stand up any longer. I slid down to the floor and crouched there. I tried to shut my mind but I kept hearing things, remembering things:

"*. . . that woman executed in York . . . Margaret something . . . two priests hanged at Tyburn, they say . . . took them in for questioning . . . put them on the rack . . . they soon talked . . .*"

They would torture the priest to make him talk. Would they torture me? If they asked me questions, would I be able to stop myself answering them? We crouched in the dark, side by side, peering into nothing.

"You're a brave girl," the priest whispered. Then he added in a low voice, so low I was hardly sure if I'd heard it or not, "Like your mother."

"Like Mother? What do you mean? Do you know Mother?"

"You're old enough to keep a secret, Judith?"

Here we were, hiding in the dark from the Queen's men who might kill us if they found us, and he was asking me if I was old enough to keep a secret. He must have realized how stupid it was, because he said, "I'm sorry. Of course you are. Yes, I knew your mother long ago, when we were children. That's how I knew who you were – you're very like her. Then we grew up and she married your father and came here, and I went abroad."

61

"She never told me anything about you."

"Perhaps she thought it was best not."

My mother seemed like a different person suddenly. She'd had friends I'd never even known she had. And they grew up together; he must have been important to her. But he became a priest. I had so many questions to ask—

Three scratches, and then the white gap in the dark. It hurt my eyes again. Matthew's voice.

"Quick. Over here."

We stumbled towards the light. It was Matthew. He pushed past me and shoved a basket and a bundle into the hole, then hauled me out. The priest let go of my hand. I looked back, but he didn't move. I could see his quiet face in the light from the panel door before Matthew shut it again and left him there alone.

"Hurry. We can get you out. All the women and children from the village are up here, round the house. They came with the soldiers. They're making sure no one escapes. Go straight down the stairs and into the kitchen. There's a guard on the main door, but if anyone sees you, say you pushed your way in. If you curse us and yell enough they'll believe you. Once you're in the stableyard you can slip into the crowd and start shouting like the rest of them. Everyone knows you."

"I shan't do that. I shan't yell and shout like them," I said angrily.

"You will. You've got to. Then no one'll guess."

And I did. I cursed the Bowmans for Papists, I shook my fist and spat and swayed and yelled with the crowd. The soldiers wanted us there, but they didn't want us to get too rough. All the village was there, but my mother and father never came. When we surged forward, the soldiers pushed us back, showing their pikes. It wasn't till nightfall that some of the crowd began to get bored and drift back to the village. After all, there was nothing to see. Mistress Bowman sick with ague. And she'd been good to many in the village in her time. She'd made medicines out of herbs, and sent wine to people who were sick. People began to remember it. They grew cold and shifted their feet and thought of home.

But I stayed. I stayed and watched it all. Three soldiers skewered live hens on their swords: Mistress Bowman's hens, whose eggs Anne had been hunting. Others lit a fire in the stableyard while James the stable-boy looked on, not daring to protest, white with fear that the stables would catch fire and the horses burn alive. The officers watched and smiled.

My mother ran out to meet me as I came in through our gate. Her face was pale.

"Where have you been, Judith?"

"Up at the Hall."

She reached out and hugged me so tight I could hear her heart bumping.

"They haven't caught him," she whispered.

"No. He's hidden. Mother—" But I didn't go on. She hadn't told me, and it was her secret.

"All the village is up there," I said. "I hate them!"

"You mustn't do that," said my mother. "They are our neighbours. We have to live with them."

They didn't find the priest that time. He crouched behind the panelling for three days while the soldiers sat in the kitchen and ate the hams and cheeses Eliza had put away for the winter, and drank all Mistress Bowman's mead and apple wine. At night they got drunk and roared out songs, keeping time with their fists and their boots. You could hear them all through the yards and the orchard and way down nearly to the village. From there people could see the fires they lit, leaping and roaring into the sky as if the Hall itself was on fire. But they didn't fire the Hall, not this time. They smashed Mistress Bowman's fine chair, and ripped her mattresses with their swords till the house was full of feathers, saying they were looking for the priest. They burnt the hen-houses and when they left they took Star with them, and they would have taken Matthew's father's mare if she hadn't been lame. I thought of how Matthew couldn't bear to knock the head of a trout against a stone, but he had to live for three days in that house with the soldiers listening for every sound, and his mother sick, and Anne whimpering with terror every time a soldier came into the room. It would keep on happening, over and over, I knew, as long as the Bowmans stayed Papist.

I saw the soldiers go. They had their packs clutched to them, full of what was left of the Bowmans' stores. And china, and glass, and everything they could carry. No matter if it smashed on the journey. I stood in the yard and watched the stragglers go. There were only a few of us from the village left now, and we didn't look at each other much. It was as if we were ashamed. I listened to their boots, going off down the lane, and stood there, watching the house. The sun was warm and the doves which were still alive were purring up on the roof. Soon the last few watchers would go back to the village, and I would knock softly on the side-door, and Matthew would let me in.

I had scarcely been home those past three days, except to eat and to sleep, but my mother knew where I was and she didn't stop me. She understood that I wanted to be where Matthew was, even if I couldn't help him. Once or twice she started to say something and I thought she was going to tell me about the boy she had known all those years ago, who was a Papist too. But it wasn't the right time. She kept her secret and I kept mine, but I knew one day we'd tell one another. The village people would say I'd betrayed them if they knew how I'd run across the fields to warn the priest and help him hide, but I knew now that my parents would be glad I'd done it. I'd kept Matthew's secret, and I could keep my mother's. I was part of it now.

You Can Do It

Theresa Breslin

"Fiona, for goodness sake, hurry up!" Her mother's voice, sharp with annoyance, sounded all the way up the stairs to the attic. Fiona scowled and stuck her chin out. She *was* hurrying, had been hurrying all day in fact. "Do this, Fiona. Take that, Fiona. Where are the drawing pins, Fiona? Bring this downstairs. Carry something back upstairs. Fetch the hammer, Fiona. Can't you be a bit quicker? Don't slouch about, Fiona. We don't have much time."

Fiona picked up the last box which she was bringing down out of the attic and, as she did so, it burst. Without warning it gave way, spewing bills and invoices, old photographs, postcards and letters all over the floor. She gazed down in bewilderment at the mess. The lid was still in her hands. It must have been so crammed full that the bottom had just fallen out.

"Blast! Blast! Blast!" She threw the lid down and kicked it across the floor.

She disliked flittings she decided as she gazed at the chaotic pile of papers at her feet, and this one she especially hated. Moving Grampa out of his big old house into one of those new antiseptic flats. There was never going to be enough space for all his things, and hardly enough room for her to stay over every weekend with him as she had done ever since she was small. As she knelt down and began to gather up some of the bits and pieces, she heard her mother's voice again.

"Fiona! Come down this minute!"

Fiona dropped the papers she had in her hand and went to the door.

"Coming," she shouted.

She trudged down the narrow attic stair and through the door on to the first landing. She could see her mother's face peering up at her from the stairwell.

"Whatever is keeping you up there?" And before Fiona had time to answer she went on. "Give me a hand with these curtains. We'll have to leave now. I don't want to have Grampa waiting too long on his own at the new flat."

Fiona walked down the next flight of stairs to the bottom hall. She passed her father on his way to the back kitchen.

"Are you going with your mum?" he asked.

Fiona shrugged. "Looks like it," she said.

She went out the front door and helped her mother bundle the curtains and some carrier bags into her car.

"You won't be able to get in here now, Fiona." Her mother clicked her tongue in exasperation. "I don't know where we're going to put all this stuff when we get there."

"Exactly," said Fiona bitterly. "This move is such a stupid idea. I said so from the beginning."

"Oh don't start again." Her mother was angry now. "We've been through all this. Your grampa isn't fit to manage that big house any more. He's in his wheelchair most of the time, and the flat is specially fitted out. It will be much better for him."

But not for me, thought Fiona. She didn't like the new flat with its small rooms, its smooth floors and low down handles. She preferred this house with its long garden, the high ceilings and ratchety stairs.

"You'll have to go with your dad," her mum was saying. "He's only got those kitchen rugs to bring. Will you remind him he said he would do the shopping before he came on?"

Fiona watched her mother drive off and then went slowly back inside. Her dad must still be tying up the rugs. She would have time to go back up to the attic and gather up the broken box. It was mainly photographs which had spilled out. One album had ended up at the foot of the attic stairs, and some loose snapshots were scattered around on the dark stained wooden floor. Memories of her grampa's life and family. There was an old one of him in uniform. She picked it up and squinted at it. He smiled out at her. A strong face with a dark moustache. Fiona sighed. He wasn't like that any more. Not since a stroke had left him with shaky legs and quivering muscles. She looked at the picture more closely. He was standing in front of a house. *This* house she realized. It seemed different. The wrought iron railings weren't there any more. She knew that they had taken them away during the War, for ammunition or guns. And that small tree . . . it must be the huge oak which grew just at the entrance gate now.

She went over to the tiny window. If she climbed up on the little ledge she could just see the topmost branches. The great mass of leaves spread a green dappled screen across the house. Fiona opened the window a fraction. From far down below in the driveway she heard the sound of a car engine starting up. She frowned. Who could it be? Her mum had already left, and there was only her dad and herself in the house.

It was her dad! That faint bang she had heard a

moment ago must have been him closing and locking the front door. And now, he was about to drive off without her, thinking that she had already gone with her mother. Fiona slammed the window down. If she was going to catch him, she would have to hurry. She twisted round and, scrambling quickly down from the ledge, she ran to the stairs.

"Those who hurry fastest are the first to fall" was one of her grampa's sayings, and it was as if she heard him saying it now, right out loud in her ear as she took the tumble on the first step. Seconds later she landed with a crash at the foot, hard against the door to the landing. She moaned as she sat there. Her head hurt, her bottom hurt, her legs throbbed painfully and, vaguely through the surging noise in her ears, Fiona heard the tyres of her dad's car scrunch on the gravel and drive away.

She was quite alone in the big empty house. She started to get up. Her legs were caught underneath her body and she tried to heave herself up and straighten them out.

"Oww," she yelped. A stabbing pain flared in her knees. She moved again, this time more carefully.

"Mmmm," she ground her teeth together. The pain was terrible, the worst she had ever suffered. Worse than when she had fallen from her bike on the driveway of Grampa's house and badly gashed her

72

leg. He had picked her up and run all the way to the
health clinic with her in his arms, and sat her on his
knee while the doctor stitched the wound, and then
given her his big hanky and told her it was all right
to cry.

Well she was going to cry now. There were tears
crowding in behind her eyelids and her hands were
shaking. She looked down at her knees, they were
swollen and puffy, and when she tried to move at all
they hurt badly.

"Now what am I going to do?" she asked herself.
She looked at the door to the landing. It had been
pushed shut by her falling against it. The handle was
higher than she could reach. She moved her legs

again but she couldn't stand up. She was a prisoner.

"Don't be daft, Fiona," she said aloud. "When Dad gets to the new flat they'll figure out what has happened and come back at once . . ." Or would they?

Both her parents were so harassed at the moment with Grampa being unwell and moving house that they might not realize she wasn't there, not for a while anyway. But then, Fiona thought, there *was* someone who usually noticed immediately that she wasn't around. Grampa.

"How's Fiona, me old mate?" was the first thing he asked whenever they came to visit him.

"Your mum and I shouldn't really bother coming along at all," her dad would tease Fiona. "It's only you he wants to talk to."

Or when Grampa used to be strong enough to come on the bus to see them. Opening their front door he would shout out, "Where's my pal?" And when Fiona was little she would run and jump up into his arms.

Fiona frowned. She couldn't do that any more. Not since his stroke . . . well, she stuck her chin out, she was now much too grown-up to act like that anyway. She pushed the thought away quickly, trying to avoid the truth, which was that Grampa with his stroke wasn't the same Grampa that she had played with before. Which is what she had told her dad when he had asked her why she didn't spend much time with Grampa now.

"Well, everybody changes as they grow older, Fiona," her dad had replied slowly. "But Grampa is still the same person, perhaps you're just not looking closely enough."

Well she didn't want to look closely. The first day he had come home from hospital she hadn't recognized the sick old man whose clothes seemed too big for him. She had pictured herself helping him get better sorting his cushions, picking flowers for his room. And he would smile and nod and say "thank you, Fiona", and then they would play cards and she would win most of the games. But it hadn't been like that at all. He sat slumped in his chair by the fire most of the day, his eyes were vague and sometimes he dribbled his food. Just like a baby!

"Fetch a cloth for Grampa," her mum had asked her. Fiona brought it, and thrusting it quickly into her mother's hand she hurried away. Her dad had spoken to her later. "Couldn't you sit with Grampa for a little while, maybe read to him?" he asked. "He needs some encouragement to get well." Fiona shook her head. "I'm busy," she said. "I've lots of school work to do for tomorrow."

She didn't want to sit on the little stool beside his chair and talk to Grampa. His eyes were always sad, and he hardly ever answered anyone anyway. "He's not even trying," Fiona's mum complained. "He's supposed to practise words and exercise his fingers, and he just sits all day."

And as the weeks passed and he didn't get much better he finally agreed to sell the big house and move closer to Fiona's mum and dad's home. "He should have done this years ago," said Fiona's mum. "That house and garden were far too much for him to keep up."

Fiona was horrified. No more hide and seek games in the big old-fashioned rooms, no attic to explore! Her weekends would be so dull in the tiny cramped new place. But when she said this to her parents they didn't seem to care. "Grampa's legs are not very strong now," her mum had said, "he can't be doing with all those stairs. There's none in the new flat. It will be much easier for him."

Fiona looked at the stairs reaching up behind her to the attic. It would be impossible for her grampa to walk up them now, even climbing to the first floor to go to bed exhausted him. And supposing he had stayed on in this house and had fallen as she had? Fiona shivered suddenly. He might have lain for hours or days, unable to reach the telephone and no one to hear him calling for help.

She looked at her watch. Why were her mum and dad taking so long? It was only ten minutes to the flat, and another ten back by car. Only . . . she suddenly remembered Dad was going to the supermarket. Fiona groaned, she might have to wait for ages before they came. She moved her position, something was pressing into her back. Something hard with sharp corners. She pulled at it. It was a photograph album. Carefully written on the front in her grampa's writing was

Fiona, growing up

Fiona made a face. She hated baby photographs of herself. Still . . . it would pass the time, and take her mind from the pain. She flicked it open. There was one of Grampa with his arm round her as she stood in the swimming pool. It seemed silly, now she was older, but she had been scared to stand by herself in the water. Her legs had trembled as she stepped away from the tiled side.

"You can do it, Fiona," Grampa's voice whispered in her ear. "You can do it." And he had placed his strong arm round her waist and steadied her until she was confident enough to stand on her own. Fiona turned the pages of the album.

There was another one, taken a year or more later. She was on a swing, hair flying out behind as Grampa pushed her higher and higher. And then he had explained to her how she could make the swing go backwards and forwards.

She smiled as she studied the picture. She had
fallen out with him, because he wanted her to do it on
her own, and refused to push her until she tried. She
had shouted and cried and said a bad word, and he
had laughed, and said she could do it herself, and
then sat on the swing alongside her to show her how
easy it was. And then they had a competition to see
who could swing the highest, and she won, of course,
and she had said "Sorry Grampa" for shouting. And
he had pulled her hair and said "What are friends
for?"

What were friends for? Helping each other she
supposed. She looked up at the doorknob above her
head. She could do with some help now . . . and so

could he, she suddenly thought.

Someone, a friend, to help him now that he had trembling legs, now that he was unsure, with no confidence, maybe a little scared of trying. Fiona felt more tears coming, and this time she didn't stop them.

And she was still tearful, with a grubby streaked face, when her dad came rushing back into the house an hour or so later.

"Fiona! Fiona!" she heard him yelling frantically as he ran up the stairs.

"You poor thing!" he cried when he saw her.

"You poor thing, Fiona." Her mother hurried out to meet her later as her dad helped her with her crutches out of the car.

"Don't fuss, Mum," said Fiona. "The hospital said it's only a bad twist."

"Sit in the living room," said her dad, "and we'll make some supper."

Grampa was sitting by the fire, hands resting on each knee. He looked up as Fiona came in. His eyes followed her as she limped slowly across the room. "Just as well you moved out of that old house," said Fiona. "Neither of us will be able to manage stairs for a while." She sat down beside him. "How about a trade," she suggested. "I borrow your wheelchair and you get a turn of my crutches?"

The old man looked at her uncertainly. Fiona giggled.

"We could have races," she said. "Bet I could go faster than you." She looked at him, full in the face, the first time she had done so since he had been in hospital.

"Where's your mirror?" she asked.

"Mirror?" he repeated.

"You're meant to have a hand mirror by your chair and do your vowel sounds every day," she said. "You've not been doing it, have you?"

He shook his head slowly.

"Well, it's not good enough," said Fiona severely. "We are going to have to make a start right away." Then she winked at him, and leaning forward close to his head she whispered in his ear.

"You can do it, Grampa. You can do it."

The Reluctant Python

Gerald Durrell

An enormous python has been spotted in the jungle and the author and his friend have decided to see if they can capture it . . .

The path lay at first through some old native farmland, where the giant trees had been felled and now lay rotting across the ground. Between these trunks a crop of cassava had been grown and harvested, and the ground allowed to lie fallow, so that the low growth of the forest – thorn bushes, convolvulus and other tangles – had swept into the clearing and covered everything with a cloak. There was always plenty of life to be seen in these abandoned farms, and as we pushed through the intricate web of undergrowth there were birds all around us. Beautiful little flycatchers hovered in the air, showing up powder-blue against the greenery; in the dim recesses of convolvulus-covered tree stumps robin-chats hopped perkily in search of grass-hoppers, and looked startlingly like English robins; a pied crow flew up from the ground ahead and flapped heavily away, crying a harsh warning; in a thicket of thorn bushes, covered with pink flowers among which zoomed big blue bees, a kurrichane thrush treated us to a waterfall of sweet song. The path wound its way through this moist, hot, waist-high undergrowth for some time, and then quite abruptly the undergrowth ended and the path led us out on to a golden grassfield, rippling with the heat haze.

Attractive though they were to look at, these grassfields were far from comfortable to walk across. The grass was tough and spiky, growing in tussocks carefully placed to trip the unwary traveller. In places, where sheets of grey rocks were exposed to the sun, the surface, sprinkled with a million tiny mica chips, sparkled and flashed in your eyes. The sun beat down upon your neck and its reflections rebounded off the glittering surface of the rock and hit you in the face with the impact of a blast furnace. We plodded across this sun-drenched expanse, the sweat pouring off us.

"I hope this damned reptile's had the sense to go to ground where there's some shade," I said to Bob. "You could fry an egg on these rocks."

Agustine, who had been padding eagerly ahead, his sarong turning from scarlet to wine-red as it absorbed the sweat from his body, turned and grinned at me, his face freckled with a mass of sweat-drops.

"Masa hot?" he inquired anxiously.

"Yes, hot too much," I answered, "'e far now dis place?"

"No, sah," he said pointing ahead, "'e dere dere . . . Masa never see dis man I done leave for watch?"

I followed his pointing finger and in the distance I could see an area where the rocks had been pushed up and rumpled, like bedclothes, by some ancient volcanic upheaval, so that they formed a miniature cliff running diagonally across the grassfield. On top of this I could see the figures of two more hunters, squatting patiently in the sun. When they saw us they rose to their feet and waved ferocious-looking spears in greeting.

"'E dere dere for hole?" yelled Agustine anxiously.

"'E dere dere," they called back.

When we reached the base of the small cliff I could quite see why the python had chosen this spot to stand at bay. The rock face had been split into a series of shallow caves, worn smooth by wind and water, each communicating with the other, and the whole series sloping slightly upwards into the cliff so that anything that lived in them would be in no danger of getting drowned in the rainy season. The mouth of each cave was about eight feet across and three feet high, which gave a snake, but not much else, room for manoeuvring. The hunters had very thoughtfully set fire to all the grass in the vicinity, in an effort to smoke the reptile out. The snake had been unaffected by this, but now we had to work in a thick layer of charcoal and feathery ash up to our ankles.

Bob and I got down on our stomachs and, shoulder to shoulder, wormed our way into the mouth of the cave to try and spot the python and map out a plan of campaign. We soon found that the cave narrowed within three or four feet of the entrance so that there was only room for one person, lying as flat as he could. After the glare of the sunshine outside, the cave seemed twice as dark as it was, and we could not see a thing. The only indication that a snake was there at all was a loud peevish hissing every time we moved. We called loudly for a torch, and when this had been unpacked and handed to us we directed its beam up the narrow passage.

Eight feet ahead of us the passage ended in a circular depression in the rock, and in this the python lay coiled, shining in the torchlight as if freshly polished. It was about fifteen feet long as far

as we could judge, and so fat that we pardoned Gargantua for comparing its girth with his enormous thigh. It was also in an extremely bad temper. The longer the torch beam played on it the more prolonged and shrill did its hisses become, until they rose to an eerie shriek. We crawled out into the sunlight again and sat up, both of us almost the same colour as our hunters because of the thick layer of dark ash adhering to our sweaty bodies.

"The thing is to get a noose round its neck, and then we can all pull like hell and drag it out," said Bob.

"Yes, but the job's going to be to *get* the noose round its neck. I don't fancy being wedged in that passage if it decided to come down it after one. There's no room to manoeuvre, and there's no room for anyone to help you if you do get entangled with it."

"Yes, that's a point," Bob admitted.

"There's only one thing to do," I said. "Agustine, go quick . . . quick and cut one fork-stick for me . . . big one . . . you hear?"

"Yes, sah," said Agustine, and whipping out his broad-bladed machete he trotted off towards the forest's edge some three hundred yards away.

"Remember," I warned Bob, "if we *do* succeed in yanking it out into the open, you can't rely on the hunters. Everyone in the Cameroons is convinced that a python is poisonous; not only do they think its bite is deadly, but they also think it can poison you with the spurs under the tail. So if we do get it out it's no good grabbing the head and expecting them to hang on to the tail. You'll have to grab one end while I grab the other, and we'll just have to hope to Heaven that they cooperate in the middle."

"That's a jolly thought," said Bob, sucking his teeth meditatively.

Presently Agustine returned, carrying a long, straight sapling with a fork at one end. On to this forked end I fastened a slip knot with some fine cord which, the manufacturers had assured me, would stand a strain of three hundredweight. Then I unravelled fifty feet or so of the cord, and handed the rest of the coil to Agustine.

"Now I go for inside, I go try put dis rope for 'e neck, eh? If I go catch 'e neck I go holla, and then all dis hunter man go pull one time. You hear?"

"I hear, sah."

"Now if I should pull," I said, as I lowered myself delicately into the carpet of ash, "for Heaven's sake don't let them pull too hard . . . I don't want the damn thing pulled on top of me."

I wriggled slowly up the cave, carrying the sapling and cord with me, the torch in my mouth. The python hissed with undiminished ferocity. Then came the delicate job of trying to push the sapling ahead of me so that I could get the dangling noose over the snake's head. I found this impossible with the torch in my mouth, for at the slightest movement the beam swept everywhere but on to the point required. I put the torch on the ground, propped it up on some rocks with the beam playing on the snake and then, with infinite care, I edged the sapling up the cave towards the reptile. The python had, of course, coiled itself into a tight knot, with the head lying in the centre of coils, so when I had got the sapling into position I had to force the snake to show its head. The only way of doing this was to prod the creature vigorously with the end of the sapling.

After the first prod the shining coils seemed to swell with rage, and there came echoing down the cave a hiss so shrill and so charged with malignancy that I almost dropped the sapling. Grasping the wood more firmly in my sweaty hand I prodded again, and was treated to another shrill exhalation of breath. Five times I prodded before my efforts were rewarded. The python's head appeared suddenly over the top of the coils, and swept towards the end of the sapling, the mouth wide open and gleaming pinkly in the torchlight. But the movement was so sudden that I had no chance to get the noose over its head. The snake struck three times, and each time I made ineffectual attempts to noose it. My chief difficulty was that I could not get close enough; I was working at the full stretch of my arm, and this, combined with the weight of the sapling, made my movements very clumsy. At last, dripping with sweat, my arms aching, I crawled out into the sunlight.

"It's no good," I said to Bob. "It keeps its head buried in its coils and only pops it out to strike . . . you don't get a real chance to noose it."

"Let me have a go," he said eagerly.

He seized the sapling and crawled into the cave. There was a long pause during which we could only see his large feet scrabbling and scraping for a foothold in the cave entrance. Presently he reappeared, cursing fluently.

"It's no good," he said. "We'll never get it with this."

"If they get us a forked stick like a shepherd's crook do you think you could get hold of a coil and pull it out?" I inquired.

"I think so," said Bob, "or at any rate I could probably make it uncoil so we can get a chance at the head."

So Agustine was once more dispatched to the forest with minute instructions as to the sort of stick we needed, and he soon returned with a twenty-foot branch at one end of which was a fish-hook-like projection.

"If you could crawl in with me and shine the torch over my shoulder, it would help," said Bob. "If I put it on the ground, I knock it over every time I move."

So we crawled into the cave together and lay there, wedged shoulder to shoulder. While I shone the torch down the tunnel, Bob slowly edged his gigantic crook towards the snake. Slowly, so as not to disturb the snake unnecessarily, he edged the hook over the top coil of the mound, settled it in place, shuffled his body into a more comfortable position and then hauled with all his strength.

The results were immediate and confusing. To our surprise the entire bulk of the snake – after a momentary resistance – slid down the cave towards us. Exhilarated, Bob shuffled backwards (thus wedging us both more tightly in the tunnel) and hauled again. The snake slid still nearer and then started to unravel. Bob hauled again, and the snake uncoiled still farther; its head and neck appeared out of the tangle and struck at us. Wedged like a couple of outsize sardines in an undersized can we had no room to move except backwards, and so we slid backwards on our stomachs as rapidly as we could. At last, to our relief, we reached a slight widening in the passage, and this allowed us more room to manoeuvre. Bob laid hold of the sapling and pulled at it grimly. He reminded me of a lanky and earnest blackbird tugging an outsize worm from its hole. The snake slid into view, hissing madly, its coils shuddering with muscular contraction as it tried to free itself of the hook round its body. Another good heave, I calculated, and Bob would have it at the mouth of the cave. I crawled out rapidly.

"Bring dat rope," I roared to the hunters, "quick . . . quick . . . rope."

They leapt to obey as Bob appeared at the cave mouth, scrambled to his feet and stepped back for the final jerk that would drag the snake out into the open where we could fall on it. But, as he stepped back, he put his foot on a loose rock which twisted under him, and he fell flat on his back. The sapling was jerked from his hands, the snake gave a mighty heave that freed its body from the hook and, with the smooth fluidity of water soaking into blotting paper, it slid into a crick in the cave wall that did not look as though it could accommodate a mouse. As the last four feet of its length were disappearing into the bowels of the earth, Bob and I fell on it and hung on like grim death. We could feel the rippling of the powerful muscles as the snake, buried deep in the rocky cleft, struggled to break our grip on its tail. Slowly, inch by inch, the smooth scales slipped through our sweaty hands, and then, suddenly, the snake was gone. From somewhere deep in the rocks came a triumphant hiss.

Covered with ash and charcoal smears, our arms and legs scraped raw, our clothes black with sweat, Bob and I sat and glared at each other, panting for breath. We were past speech.

"Ah, 'e done run, Masa," pointed out Agustine, who seemed to have a genius for underlining the obvious.

"Dat snake 'e get power too much," observed Gargantua moodily.

"No man fit hold dat snake for inside hole," said Agustine, attempting to comfort us.

"'E get plenty, plenty power," intoned Gargantua again, "'e get power pass man."

In silence I handed round the cigarettes and we squatted in the carpet of ash and smoked.

"Well," I said at last, philosophically, "we did the best we could. Let's hope for better luck next time."

Bob, however, refused to be comforted. To have had the python of his dreams so close to capture and then to lose it was almost more than he could bear. He prowled around, muttering savagely to himself, as we packed up the nets and ropes, and then followed us moodily as we set off homewards.

The sun was now low in the sky, and by the time we had crossed the grassfield and entered the abandoned farmland a greenish twilight had settled on the world. Everywhere in the moist undergrowth giant glow-worms gleamed and shuddered like sapphires, and through the warm air fireflies drifted, pulsating briefly like pink pearls against the dark undergrowth. The air was full of the evening scents, wood smoke, damp earth, the sweet smell of blossom already wet with dew. An owl called in an ancient, trembling voice, and another answered it.

The river was like a moving sheet of bronze in the twilight as we scrunched our way across the milk-white sandbank. The old man and the boy were curled up asleep in the bows of the canoe. They awoke, and in silence paddled us down the dark river. On the hill top, high above us, we could see the lamps of the house shining out, and faintly, as a background to the swish and gurgle of our paddles, we could hear the gramophone playing. A drift of small white moths enveloped the canoe as it headed towards the bank. The moon, very fragile and weak, was edging its way up through the filigree of the forest behind us, and once more the owls called, sadly, longingly, in the gloom of the trees.

Waiting for Anya

Michael Morpurgo

It is the Second World War. Jo, a shepherd's son, lives in a small village in the Pyrenees. Also in the village live the Widow Horcada and her grown-up son, Benjamin. Both of them are Jewish. Benjamin's daughter, Anya, has disappeared. While he waits, hoping against hope that she will reappear, Benjamin helps people escape the clutches of the Nazis, showing them a safe route through the mountains.

Today he's been trying to get a young Polish girl safely to Spain. But it's getting dark, there are soldiers in the mountains, and Benjamin should have been back hours ago . . .

Someone had to go and find out what had happened to them and Jo knew it would have to be him. There was no one else who could go. It was too far and too steep for Widow Horcada.

"Which way does he go?" Jo asked. "The Col de Loraille?"

"Usually," she said.

There were only a few hours of light left, he'd have to hurry. As he turned to go Widow Horcada caught him by the arm.

"You take care now, boy, d'you hear me?"

"Course," he said and he was out of the door and running.

From the field below the house he could see Hubert squatting on the rock, a hand on Rouf's neck. The sheep were spread out around him, yellow in the afternoon sun. Come the evening Hubert would drive the sheep home with Rouf. Jo had often gone off eagle-watching and left Hubert to bring them in – he'd know what to do. Jo reached the trees and made his way through them down towards the river. From there on he'd be climbing all the way. He knew the path to the Col de Loraille well. It was the route up to their high summer pastures, to Papa's hut. The trees were loud with wind and the leaves were falling all about him. He followed the tumbling river upwards. Ahead of him, when the trees allowed, he could see the circle of sharp peaks at the head of the valley and above him the clouds raced each other back towards Lescun. He thought of shouting for them but he knew it would be pointless. Nothing could be heard over the roar of the river and the gusting wind. Every now and then he'd stop to scan the hills and woods about him. He saw a deer, but that was all.

On and up he climbed until at last there were no trees above him, only the peaks and the sky. Dusk was beginning to settle. A flock of crows harried a lone buzzard towards the mountains. He looked about him for any sign of movement. There was nothing, only the buzzard and he seemed to be making for Spain, chased all the way by the marauding crows. He disappeared over the peaks and the crows seemed satisfied with that for suddenly they broke off the chase and dispersed.

The sound of the shot came a moment later, echoing around the mountains. Without that Jo would never have seen the patrol. He crouched down behind a rock. There were three of them, three tiny dark figures moving slowly along the ridge against the skyline. A few of the crows settled on the ground now by Papa's hut and it occurred to him then that if Benjamin and Léah hadn't already been caught then they might be hiding up somewhere, and in that case there would be no better place than Papa's hut. The hut was several hundred metres away from him, built against a huge rock that had tumbled down the mountainside hundreds of years before. There were boulders strewn between him and the hut, boulders

that he could use as cover; but even so he'd have to wait until the patrol had gone or until dark, whichever came first. For an hour or more the patrol moved slowly along the crest towards the Pic d'Anie and then the darkness thickened around him and he could see them no more.

The sliver of moon was for decoration only, it provided no light. It was safe enough to move now. Jo scuttled from boulder to boulder until he reached the hut. He whispered at the door as loud as he dared. "Are you in there? Anyone in there?" But the reply came from behind him, from the donkey shed, just a cave in a rock with a half door across.

"Over here, Jo. We're over here." It was Benjamin's voice.

He leapt the stream and picked his way over the rough ground towards the donkey shed.

"Inside!" said Benjamin opening the door and pulling Jo in. And then he saw Léah. She was backing away from him into the darkest corner of the shed. Benjamin limped after her leaning heavily on a stick.

"Don't mind her," he said. "She's frightened of her own shadow this one, but then she's got good cause." It was some time before she could be persuaded to come out of her corner, and even then she wouldn't look at Jo but buried her head in Benjamin's coat. "She's cold and she's tired, Jo," he said, "like me. We tried to cross last night. And we'd have made it too."

"What happened?" said Jo.

"My ankle, my confounded ankle, that's what happened." He stroked Léah's hair and hugged her close to him. "We had the perfect night for it. Lots of clouds, plenty of wind; but soldiers, soldiers everywhere. I must have been over these mountains a dozen times now and I've never seen so many soldiers. That's why we were running. We don't normally run. It's always quieter if you walk. I don't know if it was a stone or a hole in the ground, it doesn't matter anyway. Somehow or other I turned my ankle over, you could hear it go – like a gunshot it was – and now it's blown up like a balloon. Anyway, we couldn't go on any further so all day we've been cooped up in here waiting for the soldiers to go. We were going to try to make it back on our own after dark, but I don't think we'd ever have done it, not on our own."

"Is it broken?" Jo asked.

"Perhaps, but anyway it won't be much use to me for a few months, that's for sure." He bent over and kissed Léah on the top of her head. She looked up at him. "It'll get better – God willing – and when it does we'll try again. I don't care how many soldiers they put on those mountains, we'll find a way past them. Now, Jo," he said, reaching out and putting a hand on his shoulder, "I'm going to need someone strong to lean on." He turned to Léah and spoke in another language. Léah looked from Benjamin to Jo and back again. Benjamin nodded and nudged her forward. She reached out slowly and Jo took her hand. "All clear outside is it?" said Benjamin. Jo peered out. He could hear nothing and see nothing. He felt Léah's cold fingers gripping tighter.

"All clear," he said, and with Benjamin's arm hooked round his neck they walked out into the night.

It was a slow and painful journey down the mountain. Benjamin may have been a small man but he was heavy enough and Jo's shoulder ached under his weight. He had to tread very carefully for he knew that if he stumbled they would all fall like a pack of cards. Léah clung to Jo's free hand and even on the narrowest tracks nothing could persuade her to let go and follow along behind. Any sudden jolt and Jo could hear the stifled groan, and feel the grip tighten round his shoulder. They stopped to rest by the river knowing that the worst part – the uphill part – still lay ahead. From now on Benjamin needed Léah too as a crutch, but even with one hand on her shoulder and an arm round Jo he had to put some weight on his useless foot. Every step was an agony to him, an agony Jo suffered with him.

Jo took them the quickest way up the hillside, across the open fields. There was no thought in his mind now of avoiding German patrols or of meeting anyone else for that matter; and clearly Benjamin felt the same for he began to sing, softly at first, through clenched teeth, and then within moments Léah's thin piping voice joined his. It was a slow, martial song, with a simple rhythmic tune that Jo soon picked up as well. That song with its regular, defiant beat kept them going all the way up to the house and by then they were singing out loud against the wind. A shadow came out from behind the barn and became Widow Horcada.

She took Benjamin's outstretched hand. "We're all right, Grandmère," he said, "we're all right." And Jo found himself suddenly and blissfully free of Benjamin's weight as Widow Horcada put her arms round him to support him.

"I'd better be getting back," said Jo, rubbing his shoulder. "They'll be wondering."

"Bless you, Jo," said Widow Horcada. It was the first time she'd ever called him "Jo".

"I told you, didn't I?" said Benjamin. "I said this boy was a good one." He bent down and whispered something to Léah.

"*Dziękuję*, Jo" she said, and her face broke at last into a shy smile.

"What does that mean?" Jo asked.

"It means 'thank you' in Polish," said Benjamin.

The Joyous Company

Rosemary Sutcliffe

Hugh has run away from his cruel Aunt Alison, taking only his beloved dog Argos, and the periwinkle plant that his mother left him before she died. He has decided to go to Oxford to seek his fortune . . .

"We've overslept," said Hugh.

"Yee-ow!" said Argos, leaping out of the ditch and stretching first his front legs and then his back ones, and yawning so wide that Hugh could see right down his pink throat.

Hugh made sure his three-farthing bit was safe and, collecting the pot of periwinkle, scrambled out too. Just at first he was so stiff all over and his feet hurt so much that he could hardly crawl along, but after a while the stiffness and soreness wore off a little. He was very hungry too, but that did not wear off; it grew worse and worse as he trudged on down the road, until it became a dull gnawing pain in his inside. Still, he must be more than twenty miles from Aunt Alison, and Argos was safe, and at the next village they came to he meant to walk boldly in and find the parsonage and ask the way to Oxford. So when they came to a wayside pool he stopped to wash his face so that he should look tidy and respectable for the parson.

It was a very still, dark pool, rimmed round with brown-tufted rushes and water forget-me-nots, and when Hugh knelt down and bent over it, his own face looked up at him just as clearly as from a mirror; a thin, brown, dirty face, with a large curly mouth; not at all respectable. He washed it very hard to see if that would improve it, and then he washed his hands and had a drink (Argos had already had one), and brushed himself down as well as he could. Then he smoothed Argos's beautiful brindled coat so that he should look his best too, and gave the periwinkle a palm-full of water. It already looked its best, and perfectly tidy and respectable; periwinkles always do. After that they went on again.

But before they came to a village they came to an inn. A rather tumble-down hedge-tavern, with a clump of crazy outbuildings beside it, and a great bush of greenery on the end of a pole sticking out above the door for a sign. And lounging at their ease before it, with a large, black leather ale-jack

between them, were a little company of men.

The moment Hugh saw those men, he began to walk slower, and slower still; and when he came opposite to them he turned into a field-gate and stood there, pretending to do something to his shoe, and stealing shy glances at them every few moments; and then he gave up pretending altogether, and simply stood and stared at the little company before the inn. He knew that it was rude to stare, but somehow he *could* not turn his back on them and go on down the empty road. It was like being cold, and suddenly coming to a bright fire: you don't want to go on again and leave all the warmth and light behind you.

There were five of the men, and they were ragged and travel-stained and mostly rather dirty; but every one of them had little gallant touches about his tatterdemalion clothes. They had brighter eyes and clearer voices than any Hugh had known before; and altogether there was something about them that seemed to Hugh very joyous, as though they had more starshine in them than most people have.

One of them, a tall, dark, swashbuckling sort of person who seemed to be the leader, had an early rose stuck behind his ear. One was a square, merry-looking man with sparkling rings in his ears and a limp peacock's feather in his bonnet. Another, who had a melancholy expression and seemed very proud of his legs, had scarlet stockings, and rosettes (what people called "provincial roses") of tarnished tinsel ribbon on his dusty shoes; and the fourth, who seemed only a few years older than Hugh, had gold cords looped round the crown of his battered beaver hat. But the fifth man was the most splendid of them all, and instead of rings in his ears or rosettes to his shoes, he had a little bright Spanish dagger in his belt. He was lean and brown, and lithe as a wild cat, with very long arms, and his curly dark head set deep between his shoulders. His face was long too, and thin, and rather sad despite its curling laughter lines. Somehow he made Hugh think of Rahere, the King's Jester, whom his father had told him about: Rahere who had founded Saint Bartholomew's

Hospital in London and been the one person in England who was brave enough to tell Henry I when he ought to be ashamed of himself.

For a while the five went on talking among themselves and passing the ale-jack from hand to hand, without noticing Hugh at all; and then, chancing to swing round, the man with the rose behind his ear saw him.

"Hi! my young cockalorum! Will you know us again if you meet us?" called the man, grinning. "Best pull those eyes of yours back into your head before they pop clean out!"

The others laughed, but the Fifth Man touched his shoulder and said something in a low voice, and then called to Hugh, "Brother Dusty-Feet, come over here and join us."

Hugh said no word. He took a firmer hold on the pot of periwinkle, which was growing very heavy, and crossed the road with Argos padding at his heels, and stood looking up at the man hopefully, while they stood and looked down at him – and at Argos – and at the periwinkle.

"Well," said the leader, in a rich and friendly voice, "have you never seen actors before, that you stand in gateways and stare, with your eyes growing more like gooseberries every moment, and your mouth gaping wide enough to catch a cuckoo in it?"

"No, sir," said Hugh.

So that was what they were: Strolling Players! People who wandered up and down the country acting their plays in inn-yards and at the foot of market crosses. He had heard of such people, of course, but never seen them; and now he realized what a lot he had missed in not knowing them before; and he thought how splendid it would be if they were going his way and would let him travel with them.

"If you don't mind," he said, "where are you going, please?"

"Anywhere – everywhere," said the leader, with a superb flourish of his right arm. "We come and go like the wind. We follow the road to the Foot of the Rainbow – but so far we have not found any gold."

When the leader spoke about the Foot of the Rainbow; Hugh knew that he simply *must* go with them, somehow; anyhow. They were the Fortune he had been so sure would meet him on the Oxford road, and he wanted to go with them more than anything in the world. "Please let me come with you," he begged in a desperate rush. "Oh, *please!*" and waited for their answer, gazing up at the Fifth Man, while Argos wagged his tail beseechingly.

Just for a moment there was a surprised silence. The Players looked at each other, and then at Hugh, and then at each other again.

"He's rather small," said Scarlet-Stockings, doubt-fully.

"He'll grow," said the Fifth Man, "and we need another boy. Nicky's getting too big to play girls' parts much longer."

"Take what fortune sends, *I* always say," said the man with the peacock's feather.

But the man with the rose behind his ear pulled at his little pointed beard and said, "Not so fast, lads." Then he looked Hugh up and down in a considering way, and demanded, "What might your name be, Brother Dusty-Feet?"

"Hugh Copplestone, please, master."

"Well, then, Hugh Copplestone, it is not the custom of those who travel the roads to inquire into the past history of any they may chance to meet with on their – er – peregrinations. Indeed, to do so is regarded among all true Dusty-Feet as – er – a gross breach of etiquette. But if you will pardon my saying so, you are a rather small vagabond, and you don't look as if you had been one long. Would you by any chance be running away from your kind home and grieving parents?"

Hugh took a deep breath and explained about Aunt Alison meaning to have Argos knocked on the head, and how they had run away together and were travelling to Oxford to seek their fortunes. When he had finished, there was another silence, and Hugh was sickeningly afraid that they were going to turn him away; so afraid that his mouth went quite dry, and he could only stand and gaze at them, with his face growing whiter and whiter under the brown.

"Well," said the leader at last, "do we take him, lads?"

"Yes," said everybody, and "might as well," they added.

"Of course we take him," said the Fifth Man. So the leader bowed low to Hugh, doffing his bonnet with a flourish that was simply superb, and laying his other hand upon his breast. "Then, Hugh Copplestone, I have the honour to inform you that your fortune is as good as made! You have fallen into the hands of those who are the masters of their art, the – er – shining lights of their glorious profession; and ere long, with due care and attention, you shall be a master of it likewise! Why, before you can turn round, you will find yourself playing St Cecilia before Gloriana herself, as she sits on her golden throne in Greenwich Palace!"

The boy they called Nicky said admiringly, "What a liar you are, Toby."

And quite suddenly, what with hunger and bewilderment and relief – but mostly with hunger – Hugh found that the world was spinning round him

in the most uncomfortable way. He swayed a little on
his feet, and smiled a sickly sort of smile, and the
Fifth Man, who had been looking at him closely, put
out a hand quickly to steady him, and said, "You
haven't had anything to eat lately, have you, Brother
Dusty-Feet?"

Hugh shook his head carefully, and found that the
world was not going round as fast as it had been,
which was a relief. "Argos too. I've got a three-
farthing bit," he mumbled.

"Don't you worry about that," said the leader,
cheerfully. "Jonathan, take the gentlemen in and
regale them on fatted calves, while we get loaded up
and bring Saffronilla round."

So the Fifth Man marched Hugh, who was still a little unsteady on his legs, into the dark inn parlour, where a round young woman like a ripe pippin gave him a large plate of pink ham and brown bread, while Argos had a bowl of the most delicious-looking scraps all to himself on the floor, and the periwinkle shared the window sill with a pot of marigolds that belonged there.

The Fifth Man sat quietly watching, while Hugh ate until he began to be gloriously full and the world was quite steady again; then he asked, "Why were you going to Oxford, Brother Dusty-Feet?"

And Hugh told him about the New Learning, and Magdalen Tower, and all the things his father had told *him*, which he hadn't spoken about to anyone since his father died.

And the Fifth Man listened to him, with his head a little bent as though he was very interested indeed. Then he said, "We're not going to Oxford, you know." Hugh shook his head and went on eating; and the Fifth Man said, "And you mustn't believe what Toby says; we're not a Queen's Company. We're ordinary Strolling Players, acting our plays in inn-yards up and down the country; and when times are good we eat as much as we want, and when times are bad we go hungry and sleep in the ditch. Do you still want to come with us?"

111

Hugh looked up, and found the Fifth Man smiling at him so that all his thin face quirked upwards at the outer corners, in a winged sort of way; and all at once Hugh felt that he would follow the Fifth Man over the edge of the world. "Yes!" said Hugh.

So when Hugh had finished the ham they went out together into the sunlight. And there before the door was a very small tilt-cart with the ends of several planks sticking out behind, and a dappled mare half asleep in the shafts. It was a nice tilt-cart, rather rickety, but bravely scarlet, picked out with yellow; and the green canvas tilt was patched with blue so bright and joyous that it looked as if it was a patch cut from the clear sky; and the mare's dappled coat shone with grooming, her mane was plaited with golden straws, and her horse-brasses that were shaped like roses and stars and crescent moons sparkled in the sunshine. The rest of the company were gathered round, pushing odds and ends into the back of the cart or talking to the mare.

"Ah!" said the man with the rose behind his ear. "The gentlemen have fed, and the road calls us. But stay! Before we set out, you'd best know who we all are, beginning with myself, Tobias Pennifeather, devotedly your servant, the leader of this band of brethren – romantic villainy is my line. Gentleman with the die-away expression and scarlet stockings,

Jasper Nye, who plays the lead in all our pieces. This with the peacock's feather in his bonnet is Benjamin Bunsell; comic relief, the trusty henchman who falls over his own feet. This in the laced hat, Nicholas Bodkyn, our Heroine. Make a curtsey, Nicky," and Nicholas Bodkyn spread his imaginary skirts and dropped a billowing curtsey. "That's right," said Master Pennifeather, approvingly. "Lastly, at your elbow, Jonathan Whiteleafe, who plays the devil in scarlet tights, and is the best tumbler in the South Country, beside."

Then everybody was crowding round Hugh, patting him on the back and telling him that he would soon get to know which of them was which, and belting Argos in the ribs in a friendly way; and in the middle of it all he felt a hand on his shoulder, and the Fifth Man, who was Jonathan Whiteleafe, said in his ear, "I'd put the periwinkle in the back of the cart, if I were you. 'Twill be quite safe there." So they went round to the back of the tilt-cart and found a nice secure place for the periwinkle between a pile of planks, which Jonathan said were part of the stage, and a battered hamper with purple and spangles showing through the gaps in the wickerwork, which he said was a costume basket. Immediately after that Master Pennifeather gave the order to start.

"For we must be in South Molton before noon if

we're to put on a performance this afternoon," said Master Pennifeather. "And if we don't put on a performance this afternoon, we can't sup tonight. So gid-up, Saffronilla, old girl."

Nobody seemed to be at all worried about supper being so uncertain, because they were used to it. Saffronilla, who had been dozing gently where she stood, woke up and shook her head and lumbered forward; the yellow-and-scarlet wheels of the tilt-cart began to turn, squeaking blithely, and they were off. The Players trudged alongside, Master Pennifeather with a hand on Saffronilla's neck, whistling softly but very cheerfully to himself; and Jonathan and Hugh and Argos all dropped a little to the rear, beyond the soft white dustcloud (somebody always had to walk behind the cart to pick up the things that fell out). The three of them were very well contented with each other's company.

"If you get tired, you can ride on the shafts, you know," said Jonathan, looking down at Hugh after a while as they trudged along.

But Hugh had forgotten about being tired or footsore; he was too happy to bother about things like that. He was part of this lovely, joyous, disreputable company. Before him the tilt-cart lurched and rumbled, wobbled and squeaked along the deep-rutted road, the dust curling up in spirals around

Saffronilla's hooves as she clip-clopped along, and the brasses on her collar and breast-band chiming and jingling like all the bells of Elfland. The hedges were clouded with lady's-lace and flushed with campion, and the cuckoos called from the woodlands far and wide; and it really seemed to Hugh that summer had come to the world overnight.

Bicycle Thieves

Joan Lingard

"**W**hy should *I* have to have her in *my* room?" demanded Tamsy, stamping up and down the kitchen floor. "Why can't Emily? She's nearer Emily's age. It's not fair!"

"I have to study," said Emily, who was reading *Jackie* magazine. "I need peace and quiet."

"You, study?" said Ben. He was blacking his rugby boots. "That'll be the day."

Emily picked up the telephone directory from the numerous objects available on the table and threw it at him. She missed, hitting instead the cactus plant on the window sill. It toppled to the floor spilling its soil.

"Better get that cleaned up before your mother comes back," said Henry, glancing up from his book. Henry was their father. Emily did not get up. "Move!" he said.

Grumbling, she took a spoon from the drawer and

116

began to scrape up the soil from the floor. "It looks half dead, anyway."

"Daddy, why *do* I have to have her in my room?" Tamsy put her hand on his shoulder.

"Listen to Little Miss Simper," said Emily. "She can't half turn it on."

Tamsy stuck her tongue so far out that she thought she'd sprained it. She pulled it back in and sucked her cheeks together.

"You're all being horrible," said Henry mildly. "I'm ashamed of you. You'll have to show a little Christian charity to the lass."

"I don't know why you talk about Christian charity," said Ben. "When were you last in a church?"

Henry turned over a page of his book.

"You weren't keen on the idea, were you, Henry?" said Emily. "Not when Mary first mentioned it." Mary was their mother.

"Well, maybe not *keen* exactly. I feel I've got enough on my hands as it is with you lot. But what else could we do? She's the daughter of your mother's oldest friend. And, as you know, her mother asked your mother before she died if we'd take her."

Her mother had said, "I'd like Isla to be part of a warm, lively family."

"We can't go back on a promise, can we?"

"I don't know why you say 'we'," said Emily. "I'm sure she'd have been much happier staying with someone on her island. I can't see her liking it here."

The Dochertys lived in a large top floor flat in the centre of Edinburgh.

"There they are now," said Ben.

He laid aside his boots; Emily dropped the cactus plant; Tamsy stood still, on one leg, as if she were playing statues; and Henry let his book slide down on to his lap.

They heard the flat door closing and Mary saying brightly, "Here we are then, Isla. This is where we live. It's a bit of a climb up, isn't it, but you'll soon get used to it. I expect the family is in the kitchen – that's where we tend to live." Mary was speaking too brightly.

She came into the kitchen, scouring it with her eyes to see if they had done all the things they were supposed to have done in her absence. (They hadn't. Ben had washed the dishes, though not the pots, and Emily hadn't got round to drying them. And Tamsy's homework jotter lay unopened on the table in the middle of a pile of comics, coloured crayons, socks, elastic bands, pictures cut from magazines for a project she was doing in school, a ball of wool that the cat had tangled, knitting needles, library books, screwed up chocolate wrappers, a brush full of

Emily's hairs and a hairdryer, and Ben's rugby boots. Mary opened her mouth to deliver a blast then, remembering the girl who stood behind her, said, not quite as heartily as before:

"Isla, this is the family." And she stood aside so that they could see the girl. She was tall for her age – twelve and very pale and she had lank black hair held back from her narrow face by two bubblegum-pink clasps. She wore a navy-blue skirt and socks and a hand-knitted grey jersey.

Mary introduced each of them in turn. Henry jumped up at once and took her hand and said, "Welcome to Edinburgh, Isla! We're very pleased that you've come to live with us." Ben, Emily and Tamsy nodded and said, "Hello" or "Hi". The girl said nothing. Her dark eyes roamed round the kitchen then came back to rest on the floor in front of her feet.

"Well now, I expect you're hungry?" Mary broke off to say, "What have you been doing to my plant, Emily? And I've told you before that you are not to borrow my hairdryer without asking! And get those boots off the table, Ben! How many times do I have to tell you . . . ?"

"All right, all right," said Ben. "No need to go lathering on."

"I'll lather you!" Mary, remembering the girl

again, subsided. But she gave Ben a meaningful look before turning back to the newcomer. "Sit down, dear, and we'll get you some supper. We've kept you something in the oven. Clear this table, Tamsy! *At once*! It looks if you've tipped the entire contents of your schoolbag over it."

"It's not all my stuff!"

"Stop arguing! Here you are, dear, have this chair." Mary removed a pile of T-shirts and jeans which were waiting to be ironed and transferred them to the formica working-top beside the bread bin. "Emily, get Isla's supper from the oven. Would you like some juice, Isla? Apple or orange?" Isla nodded. "Apple?" asked Mary. Isla nodded.

Mary took the carton from the fridge. She shook it.

"Who put this empty carton back in the fridge?"

"Not me," said Tamsy.

"It's always not me. That mysterious person. Isla, do you know someone whose name is Not Me?" Mary laughed, but Isla stared blankly back. "It'll have to be orange juice then. Do you like orange?"

Isla nodded.

Supper, a dish of aubergines, peppers and cour-gettes, cooked with tomatoes in a casserole, and topped with cheese, looked somewhat shrivelled and dried.

"Oh dear!" said Mary. "Sorry about that, Isla. But

your bus was very late, wasn't it? I hope you like aubergines?"

Isla neither nodded nor shook her head. She fiddled about amongst the food with her knife and fork, eating very little, and drank half a glass of orange juice. Henry talked to her about her journey, or tried to, but she did not respond.

Mary said, "Why haven't you done your homework yet, Tamsy? Henry, why didn't you see she did her homework?"

"You know I don't approve of homework for nine year olds."

Isla's eyes swivelled from one to the other.

"It's only half a dozen spellings, for goodness sake! It won't kill her to do that every night. She's a rotten speller, anyway." Mary ignored Tamsy's protests. "Are you good at spelling, Isla?" she asked.

As they were now coming to expect, Isla did not answer. Mary was looking exhausted. Emily began to dry the dishes.

"By the way," said Mary, "I didn't see your bicycle down there when we came in, Ben."

"You didn't?" He shot out of the room.

"Don't tell me it's been pinched again," said Emily. "Those bicycle thieves are the limit!"

"They're horrible, those thieves," Tamsy said to Isla. "I left my bike outside for just two minutes while I ran up to get my anorak and when I went back down it was gone. They stand round the corner watching you and they wear balaclava helmets pulled down over their faces."

Isla's black eyes grew large with alarm.

"Don't tell lies, Tamsy," said her mother. "You've never seen anyone in a balaclava helmet standing round the corner."

"They could wear them. How do you know they don't?"

"But you know you can't leave your bikes even for two minutes without chaining them up," said Henry.

"The thieves tour round in vans lifting bikes," Emily explained to Isla, "and then they take them apart in secret workshops and re-assemble them and change the numbers and sell them again."

"Do you have bicycle thieves on your island?" asked Tamsy.

"Don't be silly," said Emily. "The police could easily track them down on an island."

Ben came bursting into the room, his face red with fury. "It's gone! My new bike! If I could lay my hands on them . . ." He held a severed chain. "They cut the chain." He threw it angrily on to the floor.

"That won't help." Henry sighed. "I'll have to get on to the insurance, *again*. I don't know what they're going to say. Last time they were suspicious enough.

'You seem to lose an awful lot of bicycles in your family, Mr Docherty,' they said."

"You'll have to bring your bike up the stairs in future," said Mary. "We've told you before."

"I was going to go out again to see Jim. It's a heck of a long way to carry it up and down *every* time."

"Emily carried hers up."

Emily smirked.

Isla's head was drooping over her plate.

"Come on, dear," said Mary, helping her up. "It's been a long day for you. And you, too, Tamsy, and don't start giving me all that about having homework to do – it's too late now. It'll serve you right if you get a row from your teacher."

When she came back, on her own, she sank down into a chair.

"I've been telling these two not to lay it on too thick about bicycle thieves," said Henry. "The poor lass'll probably dream about them. She'll be thinking the town's a terrible place."

"It's not us that lays it on thick," objected Emily. "It's that wee squirt of a sister."

"That's no way to talk about your sister!" Mary looked at Emily and Ben. "You will have to make an effort with Isla! You've got to remember she's going through a very difficult time."

"What can we do if she won't speak?" said Emily.

"Maybe she can't speak," suggested Ben.

"She said hello to me when I met her off the bus."

"So are you trying to say that it's us that have struck her dumb?" asked Emily.

"It's perfectly possible," said their mother.

"If she would even cry!" said Mary.

They were having one of their interminable discussions about what-to-do-about-Isla. Ben said they were interminable because they went on and on until it was time to go bed and they never came to any conclusion. Isla and Tamsy were already in bed, or supposed to be. The bumps they could hear suggested that Tamsy was practising handsprings.

Isla had been with them for a month, and during that time had not said one word that anyone had heard, except for "Hello" when Mary had met her off the bus. The headmaster and teachers at school were being very understanding and while they spoke to her they did not press her to speak in return. The guidance teacher had had two or three sessions with her and said all the things she might be expected to say like, "I expect you're missing your mother very much. I expect you're missing your island very much. I expect you're finding it very difficult to settle down with a new family. I expect you're finding the city strange." The educational psychologist had two sessions with her, also, and had said much the same things. But no matter what anyone said, Isla said nothing. She might at times nod or shake her head or lift her shoulders in a slight shrug but often the expression on her face did not change at all. She set off for school with Ben and Emily in the mornings and went inside the building but at the first opportunity slipped away.

Where she went, they did not know. Both Mary and Henry were out working all day – Mary was a chemical engineer, Henry a librarian – and neither could come out of work to go chasing her.

"I'm sure she just walks around the streets," said Emily. One of her friends had seen her when she'd been off school sick and Emily had seen her herself one day on the way to the museum on a school trip. Isla had not seen her. Isla had been walking along the other side of the road with her head bent down, looking into the basement flats. They saw her walking on their own street, staring with her great big black eyes into the basements. It was as if she could not understand how people lived below the level of the road.

She also stood at the window of her bedroom – hers and Tamsy's – and stared at the high grey block of flats across the street. Mary had tried to point out that cityscapes had their own charm, with their

different heights of roofs and different shaped
chimney pots, and church spires and towers sticking
up. And wasn't the sky beautiful when the sun was
setting above the rooftops? She and Henry took her
for walks in the Botanic Garden and through the
Queen's Park and along the foreshore at Cramond
though, perhaps, Mary said, that was not such a good
idea as the sight of the sea might make her feel more
homesick. Henry thought it would be better if she did
feel homesick, or at least if she would express it.

Tamsy hated seeing Isla standing at the bedroom
window staring out. It made her feel funny, she
complained. She wanted to move in with Emily but
Emily said no deal, she liked to have her friends in

and she didn't want *her* around listening to their conversation. Tamsy said it wasn't fair, she couldn't have her best friend Helen to stay overnight any more. She said she hated being the youngest in tho family. She said they were a horrible family. Henry said they would all have to stop arguing.

"The psychologist says she needs time," said Mary, "and lots of affection."

"How can you be affectionate to a stone wall?" asked Emily.

"Don't be so heartless! You should feel sorry for her."

"I do feel sorry for her. And you don't have to tell me what to feel!" Emily got up and left the room, slamming the door behind her.

"She's impossible at the moment. If you as much as look at her the wrong way she flies up in the air like a kite."

"It's her age," said Ben. And grinned. He was feeling cheerful as the insurance money had just come through and he was going to go round the bicycle shops the next day to look for a new one.

But before he got the chance to do that, another family cycle went missing. When Henry opened the door to the postman in the morning, he found that Emily's bicycle had gone. She had left it on the top landing the night before, chained to the railing.

"I'm sure I did, I definitely did. You saw it, Ben, didn't you?" He confirmed that he had.

Someone coming home late in the evening must have neglected to shut the bottom door properly, in spite of the fact that Ben had put up a notice printed in red saying "Bicycle thieves operating. Please make sure the door is securely shut." The flat beneath theirs was occupied by five students who came and went at all hours and were not at all careful about shutting the door, and who didn't wash the stairs, either, when it was their turn. Mary was forever chasing after them about it.

The family gathered on the landing in their dressing-gowns to stare at the black iron railings to which the bicycle had been tethered.

"It's terrible, isn't it, dear?" said Mary, turning to Isla, who had just appeared in the doorway.

Isla nodded.

It was the same evening, and Tamsy was sitting up in bed crayoning a picture of bicycle thieves with black balaclava helmets pulled down over their faces. At least it meant she didn't have to draw faces. She wasn't very good at them. Isla was standing, as usual, at the window. She had been there for ages.

"What can you see there?" asked Tamsy and leaping out of bed, went to join her at the window.

The street was lined with parked cars, vans and motorbikes on either side; it always was. Mary and Henry complained about not being able to find a space for their car even though they paid for residential parking. On Isla's island there would be very few cars, Tamsy supposed. Isla had lived in a hamlet of six cottages and had known everyone, which had its advantages and disadvantages, Mary said. It was friendly but, on the other hand, you never had any privacy.

"You'll get used to it, you know," said Tamsy. "Once you make some friends you'll like it better."

Isla did not answer. Tamsy was getting used to that and didn't let it stop her talking. She went back to bed and to her drawing.

"I'm not very good at drawing bicycles. I can't seem to make the wheels proper circles."

"Bicycle thieves!" cried Isla suddenly, and Tamsy nearly fell out of bed with shock.

She went rushing through to the kitchen shouting, "Isla's spoken! Isla's *spoken!*"

"What did she say?" asked Henry.

"Bicycle thieves."

They ran through to the bedroom. Isla was still standing by the window; she was trembling and clutching her hands together in front of her with excitement.

"Bicycle thieves," she said.

"That's fantastic," said Emily.

Henry put his arm round Isla's shoulder and asked her gently, "Did you *see* bicycle thieves?"

She nodded.

"Say yes or no."

"Yes."

"Where?"

She pointed across the road to where a blue van stood parked. "Over there."

"In the van?"

"No, the basement. Two boys went down the steps with bicycles."

"But they might be their own bicycles, Henry," said Ben.

"I've seen them before," said Isla. "With other bicycles."

"I suppose we'd better phone the police," said Mary, sounding unsure. "Just in case."

Henry made the call and the girls got dressed. Then they all went down the stairs and waited on the pavement.

Two police cars entered the street within five minutes and as they drew up the lights went off in the basement across the road. The Dochertys and Isla crossed over.

"There's someone in," Henry told the sergeant.

The sergeant and one of the constables went down the steps and banged on the door, the other two policemen remained on the pavement.

"Open up! We know there's someone in."

The door opened and a middle-aged man, whom the Dochertys had seen going up and down the street, looked out. He was wearing a brown cardigan and glasses. He didn't look like a bicycle thief.

"I was just going to bed," he protested. "I've had flu."

"If you don't mind we'd like a word with you?" said the sergeant. They went inside.

They found twelve bicycles all dismantled and done up in brown sacks. The sacks would then have been put into the blue van which was parked outside and driven off to a garage. The man was a bicycle receiver. And the two youths found hiding behind the dustbins in the back yard were bicycle thieves. They were brought up the steps, along with the receiver, their wrists handcuffed, and bundled into the police cars. The youths were wearing jeans and anoraks. "No balaclava helmets!" said Tamsy.

"A good piece of detection work, young lady," the sergeant said to Isla. "I'll come round tomorrow and take your statement."

The police cars drove off. Isla burst into tears.

"There now, love, it's all right," said Mary and put

131

her arms round her. "You've been marvellous. Let's all go upstairs and have some hot chocolate."

"And chocolate biscuits?" said Tamsy.

They sat round the table drinking the hot chocolate. "Imagine – they were across the road all the time!" said Ben. "And it took Isla to come along and see them."

"You were brill, Isla," said Emily.

"Thank you," said Isla. And smiled.

Dancing Bear

John Christopher

Following the death of his father the King, Dancing Bear was at the mercy of his jealous brother. Keen to protect him, Flavius Rufus, Master of Soldiers, sent him to a monastery outside the city where he was to pretend to be training as a priest. While there, barbarians attacked the city and the land . . .

The abbey stood on high ground, twenty miles to the east. Its church was still being built but already was larger than the Governor's palace. The main part was completed: the entrance and atrium, the long nave with columned aisles, the apse with the main altar, and the chapel to Our Lady on the north side of the apse. Men laboured on the Joseph chapel that faced it.

Abbot Marcus was small of stature, meagre looking, modest in demeanour. He was surprised to see me, knowing the funeral feast would be still in progress, but welcoming at first. Then, when he discovered the reason for my being there, he was alarmed. He was a man anxious to avoid trouble, and could not conceal his misgiving.

Despising him, I said, "You have the message from Flavius Rufus. I am to be an acolyte, and then a priest. Will you accept me, Lord Abbot?"

Looking at him I knew he would dearly have loved to say no, but refusal could lead to trouble as surely as acceptance: he feared to offend the Master of Soldiers as much as he feared my brother's wrath. For my part, I did not care if it was yea or nay. I would not go back – I had considered what Flavius Rufus had said, and though young was not a fool – but these were times which would furnish employment for anyone – a lad, even – who had a horse and sword.

He said, in his soft frail voice, "The church offers sanctuary to all who seek it. You may stay."

I nodded. "Thank you, Lord Abbot. I will attend to the stabling of my horse."

"Others will do that."

I shook my head, "It is mine, and I will see to it."

He looked at me with a harder eye. "No. You have nothing now: all is the Lord's." His eye went to the sword that hung from my belt, and he put out a hand.

"That too. We use no weapons here."

A day earlier I might have turned angrily away, but I was learning. A horse, my father had said, was nothing without a sword, and a sword was meaningless without a right arm to wield it. I would yield up the first two, for the time being. The third would get them back, when the time was ripe.

For several days I hourly waited the arrival of some messenger from the court, perhaps of my brother in person with his cronies, and laid plans to escape. I knew of the inviolability of holy sanctuary but had little faith in the Abbot's resolution to uphold it. But nothing happened, and gradually I came to feel more secure. Flavius Rufus, I guessed, had told the tale well. And there would be nearer and more powerful challenges my brother would have to meet. A novice in the abbey could wait his turn.

Though eventually, of course, that turn must come. I had found where the sword I had given up had been put, at the back of a cupboard full of old vestments and religious vessels, and in the time I had to myself I practised using it. In fact I was left on my own a great deal. The priests and the other acolytes took their cue from the Abbot: they spoke little to me, and required of me still less. It was plain I was an embarrassment, which they hoped would pass. I was not even tonsured until I asked for it. I did not think a shaven head would prevent my brother from killing me, but in the presence of others it might hold him back.

I attended at the Mass, of course, and as days turned into weeks came to know the church as I had known my father's palace. It was a pleasant building, full of the holy scent which is made from frankincense and myrrh, those gifts the Wise Men brought to the infant Jesus. And that third gift which they brought was there in plenty too. Gold dishes, gold bowls for holy water and gold ewers for the sacred wine, a gold monstrance studded with gems to contain the host, a gold and ivory staff which the Abbot carried in procession . . . When they were not in use they were kept in a chest in the Lady chapel. And in a smaller chest, high up on the wall, was the greatest treasure of all: the dish from which, it was said, Our Lord and His disciples supped at the Passover feast. Its sacredness was such that it was never displayed to the laity, and only shown to the clergy at the Easter Mass. I was curious to see it, but Easter was more than half a year away, and the thought of still being here then gave me no joy.

And yet there seemed small prospect of anything happening to take me away. I had hoped to get word from Flavius Rufus, to hear perhaps that he had found me some other less tedious sanctuary, but no word came.

What came instead were the barbarians. Rumour preceded, of towns stormed and sacked – at first a hundred miles away, then fifty, then closer. A pedlar told a tale that my brother had taken his army against them. It was followed by report of a great victory, greeted in the abbey with excitement and relief and prayers of thankfulness. Next day we had different news – of bloody defeat and a rabble of soldiers straggling home. There were more prayers, this time of supplication. And the day after that the fur-clad long-haired savages, swinging huge axes as they marched, were on us.

The abbey was in turmoil. I looked for some sign of a defence being organized, but found none. The monks buzzed about like bees without a queen. I remembered the words of Flavius Rufus: defiance under such circumstances would be a proof not of courage but foolhardiness. I took my sword up the mountain behind the church, to a cave I knew, where the entrance was largely concealed by an ancient tree. Its roof was low; I squatted there, and listened to the sounds – the roars of bloodthirsty exultation and the answering screams – that were carried to me on the wind.

The screams ended, but the din went on throughout that day and well into the night: they had found
the stores of wine and ale. I slept fitfully and woke
early, cramped and cold, hungry and thirsty. From
my concealment I saw them go at last, westwards
again, singing in time to the stamp of their feet. It
had rained in the night, and the sun was watery
through ragged cloud. I let it rise a good hour longer
before venturing down.

The scene was as I had expected: a tattered ruin of
goods and men. I made my way through it to the Lady
chapel. The chest which had held the abbey's
treasure was smashed and empty. So was the smaller
chest which had sheltered the holy dish. It had been
wrenched from the wall and lay on the ground in
splinters. The Abbot lay in front of it. Their axes had
obliterated his face; I knew him only by his robe.

I followed the barbarians, though not closely and not
in their immediate wake where all was devastated. A
mile or so on either side of the swath of destruction,
houses, even villages, had escaped unscathed, and
out of thankfulness were generous to a vagabond. I
slept that night in a comfortable bed. Next day, from
a distance, I watched them storm the palace.

It did not take long, and by late afternoon they had
moved on. They might have left a guard behind, to

hold it as a strongpoint, and I knew I should wait and watch; but could not. Sword in hand – yet knowing how little use it would be against those murderous axes – I made my way through the shattered gate, stepping over the tree they had felled and lopped to batter it down.

Here what they had not smashed or plundered they had put to the torch: there was smoke in the air still and timbers smouldered underfoot; the roof of the great hall gaped to the heavens. Here, too, there were corpses I knew well.

And one who was not yet dead, though dying. My brother lay among a heap of bodies at the far end of the hall, where the last stand had been broken. His right leg was a bloody mess, and another blow had smashed one side of his face. But he opened the eye he still possessed. He spoke in a whisper, "The little bear . . ." His riven face twisted into what could either have been a smile or a grimace of agony. "You must dance a better dance than I did, little bear."

I said, "I will," and brought him water, and watched him till he died.

II

All that was long ago.

In the wake of the barbarian onslaught, survivors

gathered. Among them was Flavius Rufus, and for ten years he ruled our war band before he fell in battle. I took over command, none challenging. I had a man's sword long before, and a man's horse.

We fought them ten years more, and twice ten years after that. At the beginning our attacks were scarcely more than gnat bites to a boar: we raided outlying camps and picked on bands of stragglers, relying on our horses to carry us quickly in and away. We skirmished only, knowing we were no match for them in the field. But as the years passed, our numbers increased and our power with it. We harried them ever more closely, and they first withdrew from their western outposts and after that, slowly and reluctantly, fell back towards the east.

It came to battles then, and victories. Twice they fled, to regroup and fight again. But in the third battle their backs were to the sea. Those that escaped were a beaten rabble, and thousands stayed to manure our fields. One such was their king. Nearby we found his hall, a wooden hut built large, and his treasure.

I did not look at it for two days: there were other things to do. The barbarians had left stores of ale too, and of the strong sweet liquor which sent them reckless into battle. I let my men loose on those, first appointing a few I could trust to guard the hall.

When at last I went there they were at their posts, a little drunk but capable. I was proud of them: the rest of the army lay stupefied in sleep.

Someone else awaited me, a bishop named Oweyn. He was a true Celt in height and red hair, but thin and puny in appearance. He had been with us the past several months, and had offered Mass before the final battle.

He greeted me in the high speech but addressed me as "Brenin", which is king in the native tongue. It was a custom which was growing, and I had grown tired of checking it. I asked him his business. He had come, he told me, to claim property which had belonged to the Church, before the savages stole it. Seeing my cold eye, he added that he was sure a ruler so mighty as I was lacked nothing in piety, either. Again, he called me Brenin.

I bade him follow me. The hall was as it had been left when they feasted before battle, the rough tables strewn with scraps of food, the rushes on the floor filthy and littered with drinking horns. The king's chamber was at the far end. It too was high-ceilinged, lit by a single window through which blew a breeze with the edge of autumn.

There were tapestries on the walls, of war and hunting scenes, several with gold wire woven through. Underfoot were skins, one from some great white beast. The royal bed was curtained and clothed in linen; its base was the chest which held the royal treasure. I pulled the mattress off, and lifted the lid. The chest was a good seven feet in length, not much less broad and high. It was more than three-quarters filled with articles in gold and silver, many ornamented with jewels.

I stood back from it, and the bishop, at my nod, began to rummage. With loving care he brought out dishes, ewers, candlesticks, a figure of the Christ bound to His cross. One thing I recognized; the monstrance that had hung before the altar in the abbey, when I was a boy.

I commanded his interest when I said so. He asked,

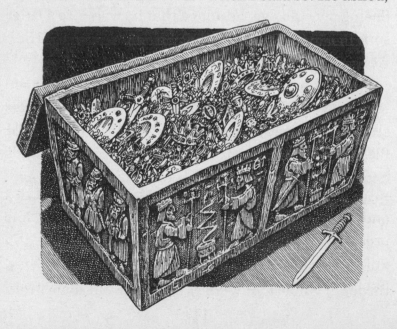

like a tremulous girl, if I had known Abbot Marcus. I told him yes.

"You are a fortunate man, sire, to have known the martyr – the saint who sacrificed his life in defence of the Holy Grail."

"But did not save it."

"He died for it. And from Heaven has guarded it, and now, through your hands, will restore it to the Church."

I remembered the scene at the abbey, all those other bodies strewn over the stone flags. Some had met harder deaths, far harder. I asked, "Do you think it is here?"

He scrabbled inside the chest, tossing costly ornaments aside in his eagerness. One was the gold torc which had been my father's. Then, with a sigh, he straightened up and turned to me again. He held a dish.

It was silver: less than two feet across, of no great substance, scratched and dented, tarnished almost black. I asked, scarcely able to believe, "Is that your Grail?"

"Yes, Brenin. This is the dish from which our Lord and His disciples ate. The blessed martyr has preserved it."

That, or plain accident. It surprised me that, having so much else more valuable, the barbarian had bothered to keep it with his treasure. He might easily have given it to his dog to drink from.

I said, "Well then, all is restored."

"This is." He cradled the dish to his bosom. "And I will guard it, God helping, with my life as he did."

"And the rest." I pointed to the gold. "I have never seen such a store of wealth."

He looked at the other things indifferently. "They are nothing; but they will be of service in the rebuilding of our churches. There is ruin everywhere."

What he said was true. We had won back our land but the years of fighting for it had left a wasteland. It was not only churches that needed rebuilding.

And to what end? We had destroyed the power of the barbarians, and those that remained must do our will. For a generation, maybe two, we might hold that governance. But in time they would rebel, and others of their race would come from across the sea; and would there then be any with a will to resist them? I thought of my satisfaction with a guard that was not too drunk to fall asleep. The ancient virtues were lost, and would not be regained.

I turned the golden torc in my hands. The empire survived in the east, but we had no contact with it: other barbarians roamed unchecked across the places between. Of the City I knew only that it had been sacked many times since that first storming. If a

Senate still existed it did so on the sufferance of its conquerors.

More than the land lay waste: customs and traditions also. The natives, to whom we had once given laws and culture, had resumed old ways: there were divisions everywhere and petty kings multiplied. It would not be an easy task to bring them together; but I must do it, even knowing that I preserved an empty shell, doomed to shatter before long.

I lifted the torc, but did not put it on. A gaudy ornament, my father had called it, and I would never wear the toga that might have dignified it. But yes, it would impress the natives, and those surviving barbarians I supposed we must call natives now. When I had accomplished what still remained to be done, I could wear it before the assembly of my subjects. They would hail me as High King, thinking it a nobler title than mere Governor.

They would think so, knowing no better.

That would be the bear's last dance. The tune I had learned as a boy had faded into silence. There were other tunes, and other dancers, but I was too old for the exercise.

Yet I could hold to the memory. And if the toga was denied me, I would manage without the bauble. I tossed the circlet of gold back into the chest. To the bishop, I said, "Take that as well. Go and build your churches."

The Trap

Martin Waddell

The man came up behind us, just as we were wandering out of the park opposite Mrs Reti's apartment. I don't think I had ever seen him before, and I have never seen him since. It is strange the way he walked into my life, changed everything with just four words, and then walked straight out of it again. I don't even remember what he looked like. He was bundled up against the cold, his face half-covered with a woolly scarf.

He thrust an envelope into my hand. "This is for you," he said. Then he was past us, striding away up the icy steps and into the park, before I had time to think.

"Lara," little Peter said, "who was that man?"

I put the envelope into my pocket, quickly.

"You must be careful all the time," Willi had warned me. *"Something may happen when you have no reason to expect it."*

"I don't know who he was," I said. "Don't stop. We've got to keep walking."

Peter is only five, seven years younger than I am, but he had sense enough to do as I said. I took his hand and hurried across the upper square, through the big doors of the apartment block, and so out of the street. I deliberately didn't look round to see if anyone was watching us.

"What did that man give you, Lara?" Peter asked.

"Don't talk to me," I said. "I need to think."

There are eight flights of stairs up to Mrs Reti's apartment, and we climbed them in silence, our steps echoing in the stairwell. No lift. Well, there is one, but it doesn't work. My Uncle Gabriel says nothing works in this country and nothing will, until we get rid of this Government. Uncle Gabriel says we will be rid of them some day.

That is what Father died for, the idea that we will be free.

That is why *they* want to catch Mother.

"It will be all right, Peter," I said. "Just trust me."

I squeezed his hand. He squeezed mine back. I was thinking: Peter is too small to be mixed up in this.

We were hiding in my Uncle Gabriel's apartment the night the Group was rounded up. Luckily, Uncle Gabriel wasn't there. Myra was looking after us. I don't know what became of Myra. They beat her, then they took her away, and we never saw her again. Willi said it was probably better not to know.

We were taken in a big car with three soldiers, and a woman. We spent the night in a hostel somewhere in the River Sector, and then they dumped us on Mrs Reti. They did not catch my Uncle Gabriel. Willi said all the others in the Group were arrested that night, all the people who were working to get rid of the Government.

So many people.

Someone betrayed them.

Someone must have.

That was one of the reasons why I didn't trust Willi. The others were arrested, Willi wasn't. Willi, with his nervous laugh and his little pills and his strange eyes. There was always a *strangeness* about him; he wasn't like the others. Everybody else taken away, but not Willi. Willi was left on the streets to buy and sell his little pills.

Why Willi? Willi was to wait, and watch us. Willi was our friend. Willi would arrange something. We were to trust Willi, he was our only hope. We were *supposed* to believe that.

Peter and I were the bait that would bring Mother or Uncle Gabriel back. That was why we were tucked away and forgotten with old Mrs Reti, half-deaf and half-blind, so that Willi could "find" us, and stage little meetings in the park, beneath the Crab Statue.

Mrs Reti's apartment was small: just four tiny rooms carved out of an older, much bigger apartment in what was once a luxury block. The walls were stud partitions across a bigger room. It meant that sound travelled very easily. Mrs Reti could hear everything that we said. She made a performance of not being able to hear, being old and frail, but I didn't trust her, and I told Peter not to. The Government sent us to Mrs Reti. The Government "allowed" Willi to find us and meet us. We had no reason to trust either of them.

I went to the bathroom as soon as I came in with the note. If I ever had to leave the apartment, I planned to do so over the domed glass roof outside the bathroom window, then down the fire escape and out at the back. That was just one of my plans for escaping, if the time ever came. The difficult thing about it was that I would have to get Peter over the roof, and he would be cold and scared.

I turned on the taps, as if I was washing, and then I sat on the toilet seat and opened the envelope.

ALL IS WELL

THE LITTLE HOUSE

16.30

It was from Uncle Gabriel.

I didn't know that from the handwriting, because

the letter wasn't handwritten. It had been typed on an old typewriter with jumpy keys. It was the "All is well". That is a kind of grim joke of Uncle Gabriel's. When he says "All is well", it means "Everything is awful, everybody panic". Like "The Little House", it was a signal that meant something to me, but would mean nothing to anyone else.

I might have burst into tears or something, but I didn't. I think I had probably used up all my tears. I was glad and happy and very frightened, all of those things muddled up. I had to plan things out, so that Willi and Mrs Reti wouldn't suspect anything.

We would go for a walk. We wouldn't take anything with us, not even Kyra, Peter's cat. We couldn't take anything, because we mustn't let anyone suspect that we would not be coming back. We would go to the Little House and Uncle Gabriel would be there, and then whatever was going to happen would happen.

It meant I had to hurt Peter. I couldn't tell him what we were doing, because he wouldn't have been able to understand about leaving the cat. Kyra had been Father's and when he was killed, Peter took the old cat over. We were going to have to leave poor Kyra behind, and I would have to betray Peter, by *not* telling him.

I had to do it. There was no choice.

I tore the note up, and flushed the little bits down the toilet.

It was four o'clock. It would take us twenty minutes to reach the Little House, and I decided that the best thing was to leave our departure to the last minute, and then just *go*. We couldn't afford to be seen standing about at the Little House, waiting for something to happen.

I came out of the toilet, and old Mrs Reti was in the hall. Her knobbly arm was braced against her stick and she was standing at the door of her room like an old witch, watching us. I am sure that she suspected something. Maybe I had been too long in the bathroom.

She was holding my scarf, the blue one that Willi gave me. Willi kept giving us little things, to cheer us up. It was supposed to fool us into thinking that he was our friend.

"Such a lovely thing, Lara," she said. "Where did you get this?"

I thought: *as if you didn't know*. Then I thought: *it was in our room*. The room I shared with Peter, at the end of the hall. She had been searching the room.

"It matches your eyes, Lara," she said, fingering it. "Beautiful! Beautiful!"

She stroked the scarf as though it were a kitten. Her hands were thin and fine, hands that were made for silk. Odd hands, to be attached to such a clumsy, lumpy old woman.

I didn't say anything.

"You are a lucky child to possess such a beautiful thing, Lara," Mrs Reti said. "Such things are not for children."

She *wanted* it. She wanted me to give it to her. She could hardly let go of it.

"May I have it, please?" I said, holding out my hand.

She gave it to me.

Perhaps it reminded her of beautiful things that she used to have, years ago, when she was little and the country was different. Now she was one of *their* spies, set to watch me. A gentle, frail old lady who loved pretty things, and a good, good friend called Willi, who brought me presents. My friends. The people I could rely on. The people who had helped to kill Father, the people who were trying to use us to trap Mother.

I put the scarf round my neck. "Peter and I are just going out for a little walk, Mrs Reti," I said.

She turned away, disappointed. I let her go, clumping her stick on the bare boards of her damp apartment.

I called Peter, and told him we were going out again. He laid Kyra down on her cushion, by the door, and came after me. I didn't speak to the cat or touch her. I couldn't. She was the last part of Father's life that we had, and we were leaving her behind.

I felt awful about the cat, and Peter, but what could I do? It was too late for me to spare time to think about Kyra . . . I had to hope that Peter would understand that when he found out.

The Little House. Uncle Gabriel used to take me there when I was little, and that is what he called it. It is a kind of cuckoo clock, only much bigger, and figures come out of it when the clock strikes the hour. He used to make up stories about it for me.

We crossed the square, and went down the steps to the road by the canal.

"I'm cold," Peter said. "Where are we going?"

"For a walk," I said.

"*Why* for a walk?"

"*Because*," I said.

"I don't want to go for a walk," he said, holding back.

"It is important, Peter," I said. "We are just going for a walk like we always do. Do you understand? Don't ask any questions. Do it."

He was great. He *did*. It made me feel even worse about Kyra, if I wasn't feeling bad enough already.

We turned the corner on to the canal bank, past

the newspaper seller. Nobody else there. Just an old woman and her dog, sniffing against a tree.

There was nothing sinister about them, nothing to make me believe that the old woman was part of what was happening, but I had to believe that, in case she was. I concentrated on the idea of Uncle Gabriel. He would come for us. He would take us to Mother. He would have to get us over the border to where she was, where we would be safe and all together again.

It was twenty past four by the clock at Mitzi's delicatessen. Ten minutes to get there. It was important not to hurry.

"Was it that note?" Peter said. "The note that man gave you?"

"Don't think about it, Peter," I said. "Just go on walking."

"Was it from Willi?" Peter said. Peter likes Willi.

"No," I said. "*Not Willi.*"

Pause.

"I don't think we will ever see Willi again," I said.

"But—"

"Don't talk now, Peter, *please*," I said. "Look at the statues."

This city has too many statues. People daub them with paint. Uncle Gabriel says it is the students. They like to annoy the authorities, to get at the

Government. There is a kind of silly statue war going on. I don't see the point in attacking statues. People who daub statues feel like heroes, but they don't risk anything. Father risked everything he had. That is why they killed him. People whose ideas are different are always dangerous.

Ideas *can* change things, if you are prepared to act on them. Painting words on walls is just a waste of paint.

There were two deep-frozen ducks squatting on the ice that covered the canal. I thought: at least *they* are not spying on us. Which sounds silly, but it shows how frightened I was.

There were four or five people standing by the railings round the Little House. We walked up to them slowly, and waited. The clock began to strike, and the doors at each side opened. The drummer came out, and the other one, the fiddler. The drummer was always my favourite in Uncle Gabriel's stories. The two figures squeaked and squealed as they came out, because no one bothers to oil their joints any more. There was the usual whirr, and the music began.

There were bird droppings encrusted on my drummer's blue and yellow wooden drum. That would have annoyed Uncle Gabriel!

"Get in the van, Lara," a woman said. "Now!"

Another one I didn't know. Not Uncle Gabriel, so that hope died in me.

"Come on!" she said, grabbing Peter's arm. The van was parked by the kerb, just beyond the clock. The woman opened the back doors of the van, and we got in. She climbed in the front and started the engine, and off we went.

Just like that. So *easy*.

The woman told us to climb under the rugs in the back of the van, and we did. I held on to Peter, closed my eyes, and tried to think.

It seemed too easy. *Much* too easy. As if it was all being allowed to happen: that thought played in my

mind. We had been sent to stay with an old deaf woman, encouraged to trust our Willi, and now we were being *allowed* to escape, picked up off the street in broad daylight with no one watching us or following us.

Peter was shivering. I couldn't see him, but I could feel his small body curled against mine beneath the heavy rugs.

"I'm sorry about Kyra, Peter," I said, and he started to cry.

We lay for a long time like that.

The van didn't stop once. That was unusual too. Normally there are police blocks round the Central Zone, and we must have passed them. Maybe it was just luck, and they had waved us through . . . or maybe *they* wanted us to get through.

The woman didn't speak to us once. She seemed to be very frightened. She wasn't a woman really, just a girl – perhaps seventeen or eighteen, not much older than me. One of my Uncle Gabriel's friends, probably.

I don't know how long the ride went on. We had to slow down twice – that may have been the road blocks – and we bumped a lot over something that I thought might have been one of the old wooden bridges of the East Sector. But otherwise I had no idea where we were, or where we were going. We lay huddled up against each other, warm but not cosy, because the back of the van had old tools and things in it which poked into us, and we couldn't straighten out properly.

Then the van stopped and someone opened the back doors and pulled the rug off and it was Uncle Gabriel!

I have never been so relieved in my whole life. It was wonderful! He had Peter up in his arms and he was hugging me at the same time and I was crying.

Then he said, "We haven't much time."

We were in some kind of old grey-stone courtyard. There had been a farmhouse, but what was left of it was falling to pieces, with sacking stuffed in the broken window frames. My uncle didn't explain anything to us. He led us into a barn and told us to hide there, and someone would come for us.

Peter started crying again.

"You'll see your mother soon, little one!" Uncle Gabriel said. He told me to keep Peter quiet, and said we were to hide amongst the old oil drums at the back of the barn and we weren't to come out until somebody came in the yard and whistled. Then he and the girl went.

We got in between the drums. I couldn't think what we were hiding from. There was no one there to see us. There were cracks in the rusty tin of the barn so we could see out, and all there was were frozen fields, flat, flat fields, and a dirt track that led away from the farmhouse towards a dark green forest of pine trees.

We lay there for ages. We talked a bit, and then we didn't. Peter curled up, clutching his knees, and in the end he went to sleep. He looked horribly tired and although I wanted to say things to make him feel better about losing Kyra, I didn't. I let him sleep.

Then someone whistled. I wriggled out, dragging Peter with me.

"Lara!" he said. "My little Lara!"

It was Willi

I didn't know what to do. I didn't trust him. I had

reason not to trust him. Willi, who wasn't arrested when everyone else was. Willi who "found" us, and brought us presents, and tried to pretend he was our friend. Willi, who was trying to help *them* to catch Mother and Uncle Gabriel.

Then I thought: *no wonder it was so easy up to now*. It was easy because Willi had made sure that it would be. He had betrayed my Uncle Gabriel, he had betrayed everyone in the Group. Our "escape" wasn't an escape at all. We were the bait in a trap to catch Mother.

I stood there staring at him, not knowing what to do.

"It is going to be all right, Lara," he said. "Don't look so frightened. Just a little walk as far as the frontier, and it will be all right. Your mother will be waiting for us, to take you over."

"Yes," I said.

"Come on, Peter!" Willi said, and Peter ran to him.

"And my uncle?" I asked.

"Gabriel?" he said. "Gabriel too. Tonight you will all be together," and he bounced Peter in his arms.

Nice Willi. Kind Willi. Good Willi. Willi watching me, not knowing that I knew. And he had a knife. It was in his belt. I wondered if I could get his knife.

"I don't want to go without Uncle Gabriel, and his friend," I said, slowly.

"Gabriel has gone another way," he said. "We must go alone."

"But—"

"Those are Gabriel's orders," Willi said. "You are to go with me."

"Come on, Lara!" Peter said.

"You must trust me, Lara!" Willi said.

I made up my mind. I didn't trust him, but he must not know that. If he did, he might do something awful to Peter. I would have to get his knife, somehow.

We left the farm. Willi led us along the wall of the old house, beckoning me to keep close in behind him, and holding on to Peter. Then he took us through a broken gate. We were in the flat, frozen grey fields.

"Quickly now!" he said, and he picked Peter up and began to run.

He ran crouching, with Peter slung round his body, and I ran too, although it didn't seem to make sense. We were moving towards the forest, and it was dusk, and whether we were doubled up or not didn't seem to make any difference.

If there was anyone there to see us, they would see us. But they wouldn't *do* anything until we were all together, Peter and I and my Uncle Gabriel, and Mother. Then Willi would give the signal. Then . . .

I couldn't think about *then*. Then wasn't going to happen. I wasn't going to let it happen.

161

Willi had fooled Father and Uncle Gabriel and betrayed the Group, and now he was using us to lure Mother into his trap.

We crossed the frozen fields and made our way in among the trees. We scrambled down into a drainage ditch, where Willi stopped, signalling me to lie down on the pine needles.

"Not far to go now," Willi said. "Just rest a bit, Lara."

I couldn't get at his knife, but there were fallen branches all around. If I hit him with a branch . . . I am not very strong. It would have to be the knife, somehow.

"I will take a look ahead," he said, and he moved on through the trees.

I let him go.

"I've cut my knee!" Peter said.

He had. There was blood right down his thin leg, soaking through his jeans. I still had Willi's blue silk scarf; I didn't want anything that belonged to Willi, but at least it was going to come in useful. I made it into a fine silk bandage for Peter's knee.

Bandaging Peter gave me time to think. I couldn't get Willi's knife, so I couldn't kill him and stop what was happening. Probably I couldn't have done that anyway. I have never killed anybody. I don't know if I could, but I would have tried then if I'd had to.

I didn't have to.

Willi had made a mistake, leaving us. I knew he must have gone to make sure that his reception committee was there, up ahead, with their guns loaded ready to move in, once they had us all together. Willi would give the sign, and they would open fire. I would be dead. Peter would be dead. Uncle Gabriel would be dead. Mother would be dead. Just like Father.

It wasn't going to happen. It wasn't going to happen because Peter and I were the bait for the trap, and we weren't going to be there!

Peter and I were going to disappear, make our own way over the crunchy pine needles and through the dark trees. I suppose I had a notion that we might somehow find the frontier, wherever it was, and sneak across all by ourselves and warn Mother and Uncle Gabriel.

"Come on, Peter," I said.

"I'm waiting for Willi," he said.

"Willi isn't your friend," I said. "Willi wants to kill us."

Peter gaped at me.

"Like the babes in the wood, Peter," I said. He knows that story. Only the robber *didn't* kill the babes in the wood. Well, Willi wasn't going to kill anybody either!

"You are coming with me, *now*," I said.

I led him away. I didn't know where I was going. I didn't even know what a frontier looked like. I had an idea that it might have a big fence and guard dogs and things like that, but there didn't seem to be a fence. Just trees, and dead silence, and twigs that threatened to snap when they cut against us, and the soft rotten wood of fallen branches and the dark purple sky that we could see through the tops of the trees. Nothing to guide us except that we were moving away from the direction Willi had gone, where his friends were waiting with their guns.

We didn't get much further.

There was another ditch, and someone was moving in it, padding along in the darkness. Three, four, five men. One after another, way down below us at the bottom of a slope. Crouching in their ditch, watching, waiting.

Willi's Trap.

We hadn't walked away from it. We'd walked straight into it. Except that we'd come from the wrong direction. We were *behind* them, not on the path where they had expected us to be.

Then somebody came down the path, and called to the men in the ditch, and they clambered out and joined him. Their leader was giving orders to the gun squad below, men in uniform who had come to kill us, and I knew their leader's voice.

It was the same kind voice that had told me stories years ago about the Little House, and the drummer with the blue and yellow wooden drum . . . wonderful stories.

Gabriel. My Uncle Gabriel.

"Don't move, Lara!" Willi said.

He pushed us both down on the soft moss of the bank above the ditch. He must have been scared when he found we were gone, but he had found us somehow.

Willi was muttering curses about my uncle. At first I didn't understand what he was saying, but then I did. It was Uncle Gabriel's trap, not Willi's. It was my uncle who had betrayed the Group. Willi had been fooled into carrying out the plan to trap Mother. That was why the meetings at the Crab Statue had been so easily arranged, why we had been put in the care of poor old Mrs Reti. The pick-up in broad daylight, the van that nobody stopped. Uncle Gabriel had arranged everything, just like one of his drummer-boy stories. He would somehow have "escaped" the ambush when it was all over. But Willi wouldn't, and neither would we, or Mother.

I know that now. I didn't know it all then, and Willi didn't try to explain. He made us go the way we had to go, to the frontier.

We went the way Willi showed us, but we could never have got past them and over the frontier, if Willi hadn't done what he did then.

The frontier wasn't there, not really. There were no fences or look-out posts. It was just a little stream through the woods. Willi told us to work our way across the stream, lower down, then down a slope to a road, where Mother would be waiting for his signal – the expected signal which would never come, now.

But there was another signal . . .

The shooting began while we were still in the trees, but they weren't shooting at us. They were shooting at Willi. He had led them away from the point where we crossed the stream. He showed himself to them deliberately, so that Peter and I could escape. We heard shots, and later more shots, then a faint cry, and then nothing.

The shots *were* a signal, to Mother, and she understood it. Willi's death allowed us to escape, and stopped Mother from coming into the wood, into Uncle Gabriel's trap.

I still have the blue scarf Willi gave me.

Mother has cleaned it, so that there is no blood.

I will keep it always, because of Willi.

The Unbeliever

Elisabeth MacIntyre

I didn't want to go to a deserted graveyard alone, at midnight, to prove that there were no such things as ghosts. I'm not the sort of chap who would stick his neck out about anything, and it's the last thing I would have chosen to do. But when you're staying for the first time with people – particularly if they are cousins who don't seem to like you very much – you do things you'd normally be afraid to – just to prove that you're not afraid.

We went swimming on the first morning after I arrived. It was fun in a deep water-hole in the creek that wound its way through the green river-flats at the bottom of the horse paddock. Then we baked in the sun to dry off – David, my eldest cousin, back from boarding school for the summer holidays – and Susan and Bill, who still did Correspondence School lessons at home.

Most of my life has been spent in different parts of

the world. Dad is a scientist. We have lived wherever he has been sent. Travel! Foreign countries! Exotic lifestyles! . . . Oh it *sounds* wonderful – but in actual fact it's awful. International airports that all look the same. Waiting around in hotel rooms while your parents attend receptions and conferences. Not having any friends. Never fitting in anywhere. In my loneliest moments I liked to think of my cousins in Australia. I had photographs of them. Knew all about them. And I'd taken it for granted that they would like me as much as I was ready to like them. But things didn't work out that way. There they were – three against one; all showing that they didn't think much of me. Oh, they were polite enough – that was the trouble, they were too polite; speaking to me as if I were a foreigner, an outsider – a rather dopey one, at that.

We talked for a while. Then silence. Everyone seemed to be wondering what to say. I was propped up on one elbow, looking back at the homestead and outbuildings sprawled over the hillside. A strange house, it looked all wrong out in the middle of a sheep-grazing property. The garden, all tangled and overgrown, was swept sideways by the winds, making it like a barrier holding the house apart from the rest of the world. Sinister-looking, I thought – but of course I didn't tell them that. Just for something to say, I remarked that they were lucky to be living in such an unusual place.

I was really surprised when David snapped, "Call that lucky? It's a bit too unusual, for my liking!"

Up till then it had been peaceful, lying on the grass under the willows. Birds chirped and chattered overhead. Horses grazed nearby, flicking their tails at the flies. I'd felt lazy and relaxed. Then there was this odd feeling that Something Awful was about to happen. Everything looked just the same as before – but felt different, then.

"We thought it would be lovely to live in a great big house with a barn and coach-house and stables and everything," Susan was more friendly now. "We didn't believe what people said about it. But . . ." she took a big breath. "All sorts of strange things have happened since we came here. The place really *is* haunted – by a mean and horrible ghost."

I laughed and said that there weren't any such things as ghosts. That's one thing I felt quite sure of, owing to my father having talked a lot about UFOs and all that. Then, seeing the looks on their faces, I quickly went on, "Dad says there's a simple scientific explanation to everything . . . He's a scientist, and he ought to know."

"He *ought* to know!"

Susan and Bill grinned when David repeated my words to make it sound as if Dad ought to know better.

"He jolly well *does* know!" I was tired of those country bumpkins who'd been trying to put me down ever since we'd met, and was determined to stand up for the one thing I really did feel sure of. "He says there are chemical substances that react against others in certain circumstances; and when they're not able to explain strange sights, uneducated people make up stories to—"

"Uneducated! I LIKE THAT!" Susan's dark hair had dripped in rat's tails around her face and I liked her then; she looked like an angry little witch as she turned on me and spoke furiously. "Just because we aren't pompous know-alls who . . ."

David threw a towel over her head and told her to shut up. "Don't take any notice of her," he said. "She's upset. We all are . . . This place had been empty for a long time when Dad bought it. There were stories of weird goings-on, but we didn't take any notice of them. We were like you then – we thought there was a sensible explanation for everything . . ."

"The house was built on land granted to one of the earliest settlers," Susan recited like a lesson. "He was determined to build a beautiful place – larger, richer, and more elegant than any homestead in the Colony. He didn't care how cruelly the convicts were treated as long as he got what he wanted."

"There's a tree behind the old coach-house, with

iron rings where convicts were chained up and flogged," Bill spoke in a scared whisper, emphasizing the awfulness of what he was saying. "And no grass grows there – even to this day!"

"Over there is the ruins of an old church," David pointed to trees over on the other side of the hill behind the homestead. "The man was mean and cruel and greedy, but liked to make it look as if he always did the right thing . . . They used to have to travel for days to get to the nearest town; and, so that nobody missed going to church on Sundays, he had one built for his family, and the servants and convicts who worked on the place . . ."

"Even then he had to be horrible too," Susan chipped in. "Just think! Underneath the church he had a dark clammy dungeon down in the ground where he could lock up the convicts when they'd been bad and . . ."

"And they probably hadn't done anything worse than fall down when the heavy stones were too much for them to carry," David said. "Even now, people tell you how much he was hated by everyone who worked for him. That's why there's that strange brooding sort of atmosphere about the place . . . Oh it's all very well to smile in that superior way – we did, when we first came here. But we know now, it's true. There's a curse on the place."

"We'll show you!" Bill jumped up, all ready to lead the way. "I bet you're not game to go down into the dungeon alone!"

I didn't want to see it. And didn't feel game to go down into any sort of a dungeon. But they didn't wait to see what I wanted to do. So we went.

We walked, single file, up the hill through tall straw-coloured grass that snapped when you trod on it, leaving a path like the wake of a ship. It was hot. The sun beat down from the wide blue dome above – it seems to me that there's *more* sky in Australia than anywhere else. Snakes? I didn't dare look down in

172

case I saw one. There's no doubt about it – my cousins are odd. Fancy being scared of something like a curse on the place – and yet walk unconcerned through a paddock which, for all we know, was alive with death adders.

We trudged over the side of the hill, near the overgrown orchard. Then down through a belt of scrub between the trunks of tall bluegums meeting high overhead like a roof. It was cooler here. Green, like a jungle. Tree-ferns, gnarled banksia bushes; and spiky, prickly plants that scratched as you passed. Then we came to a clearing, and saw what remained of the church. The front wall with its arched doorway was still standing. The side walls and roof had crumbled away. You could still see the pews. A heap of stones overgrown with blackberries showed where the pulpit used to be. A flock of brilliant parrots flashed by; and, as we went up the aisle, a rabbit ran past and disappeared into long grass behind the altar.

At a flight of stone steps, all overgrown with ferns, David stopped, and grinned as he said, "Want to go down?"

I certainly didn't want to. I'm not exactly scared of it – but I don't *like* the dark. I wasn't going to let them think I was afraid, so I stepped forward . . .

Then leapt back at the sight of an evil-looking

reptile gazing up at me; its long blue tongue darting in and out like the flick of a whip.

The way Susan laughed was enough to make me walk past a dozen of them. "Don't say you're scared of a *blue-tongue lizard*!" she said. "*Everyone* knows they're the *friendliest* old things!"

So I went forward again. Feeling along the clammy stone wall, went down into the gloom. The echo of my footsteps sounded as if there was someone following close behind – yet the voices outside sounded far off in the distance. I had to stoop to climb over a broken door torn off its hinges. And had to keep stooping, the ceiling inside was no higher than a hand-rail. Until this, a little light had seeped in. Now, taking a sharp turn right, nothing could be seen in the thick velvety darkness.

I was quite sure then, there were no such things as ghosts. I *knew* it was all in my mind – the faint whispering and sighing sounds; the figures I seemed to see hunched up in the dark. And, worst of all, the feeling that hands were stretched out, to drag me further in there amongst them . . . Just *imagination*, I kept telling myself. even so, I was scared stiff. I longed to scream. To race out into the sunlight . . . But the thought of the three of them out there, all ready to laugh at my change of attitude towards ghosts, held me back. You see, I really *did* believe what Dad had said about there being a simple scientific explanation to everything.

So I made myself stay there in the dark while I counted a hundred – fast! Then, not so quickly as they'd guess how scared I'd been, went back up the steps to where my cousins waited. It took a few moments for my eyes to get used to the bright light outside . . . Then had the satisfaction of seeing respectful looks on their faces.

"No wonder the convicts hated him! *I'd* hate anyone who shut me up in a place like that!" I was proud of myself for playing it so cool.

"They hated, loathed and detested him," Susan said solemnly. "That's why they murdered him. Battered him to death with their manacles and leg-irons."

"They did unspeakable things to his body," Bill spoke with satisfaction.

"What sort of things?"

"*Unspeakable!*" Bill shook his head. "That's why nobody will speak about them."

Out in the church-yard, David pointed to a small plot surrounded by iron railings, almost hidden in the long grass.

"That's where his grave is – he still haunts it. His headstone is lying on the ground because the ghost pushed it over."

Out in the sunshine everything seemed sensible

again. Magpies carolled in the trees; an aeroplane zoomed high overhead. I was able to smile then, at the scary feeling in the darkness – it seemed that some of their superstition had rubbed off on me.

My father is one of the top scientists in the world. He really does seem to know what he is talking about; of course I believed him. *Refuse to be fooled*, he always said. *Examine the facts, and you'll always find a simple scientific explanation*. Well, it seemed, all I had to do was examine them, and find it.

I pointed to the heavy tombstone, to big for even a strong man to push around. "Some ghost!"

David glared at it and at me.

"I know you don't believe us," he said. "But why isn't the stone upright, like the others?

Then I really annoyed them, I know; by speaking in the superior way that Dad does, when he doesn't want to hear any more on a subject.

"I definitely believe there's a simple, scientific explanation."

"And we definitely believe there's a ghost," Susan mimicked. "If you're so sure there's no such thing – why don't you find out what it *is*?"

David and Bill agreed with her.

Then David made a fair offer. "Come here at midnight tonight," he said. "If you can explain whatever it is, scientifically, we'll stop believing there's a jinx on the place. Won't we, kids?"

Susan nodded. She's a nice sensible girl, and I could see how much happier she'd be when she knew for sure there was nothing to be afraid of.

"It's scary, feeling the place is haunted," she said. "When you think there's the ghost of a horrible man around, you start imagining horrible happenings – even in things that are quite all right."

I laughed when young Bill eyed me shrewdly, and asked the others how they'd know that I really *had* gone there at midnight. "Mark could just *say* he'd been," he said. "I know *I* would."

Why had I gone and started it all? Why hadn't I kept my big mouth shut? It was too late to back out then. And besides, Dad would be interested if I made some scientific discovery . . . So I took out my notebook. Thought for a while. Wrote in it. Then tore out the page and handed it to David.

"There. Sign this . . . We'll stick it on the fence now, and I'll get it tonight. Will that do you?"

They all read:

> *We, the undersigned, all agree to agree*
> *there are no such things as ghosts,*
> *if Mark Milford can satisfy us*
> *with a simple scientific explanation*
> *after examining this grave at midnight.*

Signed, it looked impressive. David was about to stick it on one of the spear-like iron railings surrounding the grave. Then had a better idea. He put the paper as far inside the railings as he could reach; then placed a stone on top.

"There! If you say there's nothing wrong when you come back with that," he said, "we'll believe you."

"OK," I said, hoping I sounded more confident than I felt.

A whirring noise, then a deep BONG came from the old-fashioned clock on the kitchen mantlepiece when I slipped out the door at a quarter-to-twelve that night.

It was a full moon. Almost as bright as day. But things looked different. Dramatic, like a stage-setting. I had a strangely unreal feeling as if I were acting in a horror movie as I tiptoed across the courtyard. One of the sheepdogs started barking when I passed the kennels. That set them all off, barking and yelping and rattling their chains like a pack of bloodhounds after escaped convicts . . . Convicts . . . Again there was this eerie feeling of their presence I had felt in the dungeon . . . As if I had travelled back through time. The moonlight was bright as silver; but the shadows – great caves of darkness, seemed alive with wraithlike figures shuffling about. I could have sworn I saw tired-looking men dressed in garments marked with broad arrows . . . Then I rubbed my eyes and took a hold on myself. In that state of mind your imagination goes crazy.

David had shown me the shortest way. Down the back drive and along the road to a double row of pine trees leading up to the church. I hurried, determined not to look at anything, or think of anything but getting there and back as quickly as I could. I ran all the way down the drive. And along the road until . . .

Suddenly, something made me stop . . .

Again I had this overpowering feeling of being back in the past. There was a low murmuring sound. In the shadows ahead I could see things moving . . . Slowly . . . The way convicts would, after back-breaking work moving huge slabs of stone . . .

This time, I really *was* scared! I could feel the fear, like a load of ice on my shoulders, seeping down my spine. I tried to turn and run; but couldn't move – couldn't scream, even.

Then there was a gentle "moo" ahead, and a recognizable shape moved out into the half-light.

That shows you can be fooled by anything – even a few harmless cows, grazing on a country road!

I had proved, twice, that you see what you expect to see. But even so – I was jumpy now; I was seeing too many strange things.

The double row of pine trees leading up to the church made a dark tunnel. I would rather not have to go through it. But, as I kept reminding myself, I had proved there was nothing to be afraid of – so why was I afraid?

A rusty lock held the gate shut fast. It lurched sideways when I climbed it, spilling me over onto a bed of pine-needles . . . Then, what did I imagine – and what was real? It all seemed far too real. Mocking voices behind. Menacing branches stretching out in front, as if to warn me – hold me back from some horrible Presence waiting in the darkness ahead.

Was I glad to come out into the clearing around the old church-yard! We had approached it from the other side before. I stood there, looking around for where the grave would be . . .

Then stared, petrified. This time, sure of what I saw.

All was deathly quiet. And *still*. Not a thing moved. It was as if everything – including me – was turned to stone. Everything, except for the wild movement inside those railings with the fallen tombstone. White wraithlike shapes seemed to be struggling, fighting to get free.

A feeling of dread swept over me like a great wave. I longed to escape from the evil atmosphere. Honestly, I could *feel* it, like clammy air pressing in

on me all around.

I shut my eyes tight. Then, after the first moments of panic, began to think clearly again. I thought of Dad. I felt he was beside me. Could even hear the amused tone in his voice when talking about things like this: *Don't be fooled*, he seemed to be saying, *Remember! There's a scientific explanation for everything!*

I felt better then. When you're expecting to see a ghost, everything white seems ghostly. When you stop to analyse it, you see how mistaken you can be.

I saw, then, that this wasn't the right shape for a ghost. Too short, for one thing; and no head, arms, or body. Just two white spirals rising out of the ground

. . . Probably underground gas which vapourized when forced up into the cooler atmosphere.

Even so, I felt sick with fear. But determined to go through with it now. I didn't dare look at the strange apparition. Just darted forward, flopped down on my knees, and reached through the railings for the piece of paper . . .

Further . . . Further . . . Whatever it was, brushed against me. I felt it, soft and clammy. No time to worry about what it *was*. I stretched, even further forward. Grabbed the paper. Leapt backwards. Then turned and ran for my life . . .

Ran. *Ran!* Ran as if a pack of demons were behind me. Stumbling over graves hidden in the long grass, I raced through the church-yard, down the dark avenue of pines. Clambered over the gate again, hurried back along the road, up the driveway and across the courtyard; not slackening my pace until I was safely inside the house.

"Good on you! I hear you've laid our ghost!" Uncle Dick beamed at me from the head of the table when I hurried in, late for breakfast next morning.

I was pleased, but made little of it. I didn't want to seem boastful. And besides, I was hungry; so went over and helped myself from a dish of grilled chops on the massive cedar sideboard. Sun streamed in the

French windows, curtains billowed in the breeze. Everything so solid and sensible in the daylight. The happenings of the night before seemed light-years away. So far I had only told my cousins that the graveyard wasn't haunted. Later I would explain how, at first, I was fooled by what seemed a ghostly apparition. Then realizing it wasn't even the shape of a ghost, I deduced that hot air, vapourized, and separated by the fallen tombstone, would rise in two columns that could be mistaken for *anything*, by anyone with imagination.

Busy eating, and thinking what I was going to tell them, I didn't pay much attention to what was being said at the breakfast table.

Then suddenly I realized what Uncle Dick was saying.

I stopped, stared. Then a wave of horror froze over me as I pictured what I'd seen at the graveyard, and realized what it *was*:

". . . he left instructions to be buried standing. They did so – but got even with him in the end. They buried him *standing on his head!* . . . It's all such a long time ago now – it seems as if the ghost has disappeared. But, for years afterwards, people swore they'd seen his ghost trying to get out. Just two legs, they said, straining and struggling to get free."

I opened my mouth, ready to tell . . .

Then decided not to. They seemed so happy to think the ghost had left the place. As Susan said, "When you think there's the ghost of a horrible man around, you start imagining horrible happenings – even in things that are quite all right."

I know now, just how it feels.

Daddy-Long-Legs

Robert Westall

Granda's house was much too close to Hitler. The only people in Garmouth who lived closer than us were the lighthouse-keepers on the end of the piers. All there was between us and Hitler was the North Sea. On sunny evenings I used to watch the little white fat clouds blowing eastward, and think that by morning they would be looking down on places in Norway and Denmark and Holland where grey soldiers strutted around doing the goose-step in their jackboots, and people crept about in fear of a hand on their shoulder. I even worried about the clouds a bit.

We were on a tiny headland that jutted out into the mouth of the Tyne. Not worth defending, the soldiers from the Castle said, as they laid their long corkscrews of barbed wire inland from us. There was a checkpoint a hundred yards away up the pier road, where sometimes, with bayonets fixed to the rifles on their shoulders, they demanded to see our identity cards. But usually they let us through with a wink and a thumbs-up, because they knew us.

The Old Coastguard House, they called my grandfather's house. It was really only a white-painted cottage, with a little tower one storey higher than the roof. The tower had great windows, watching the Tyne on the right, the bay of Prior's Haven on the left, and the Castle beyond, and the North Sea in front. My granda had stuck great criss-crosses of sticky tape over the windows, to save us being cut to bits by flying glass if a bomb fell near. He had scrounged a lot of sandbags from the soldiers, in exchange for the odd bottle of my grandmother's elderberry wine. The soldiers were very keen on my grandmother's elderberry. They said a nip of it was as good as a tot of whisky when you were freezing on guard-duty of a winter's night. My granda filled the sandbags with soil from the garden, leaving a great hole which filled with water when it rained in winter. My grandfather considered keeping ducks on it, but he thought the firing of the Castle guns would scare them witless during air-raids, and besides, the pond dried out completely in summer. A pity, because the ducks' eggs would have helped the war effort.

My grandfather built up the sandbags round the windows of the cottage, till we looked a real fortress.

Of course he couldn't sandbag the tower windows, they were too high up. But nobody was supposed to go up there during air-raids.

I think people worried about us, stuck out there on our little headland. They offered us an Anderson air-raid shelter for the garden; but Granda said he preferred our cellar, which had walls three feet thick. They offered to evacuate us altogether. But Granda said he wasn't going to run away from Hitler, into some council house. He would face Hitler where he stood; and he ran up the Union Jack on our flagpole every morning to prove it. He and I did it together, standing to attention, then we saluted the flag and Granda said, "God save the King", without fail. Grandma said we should take it down during air-raids, as it would make us a target. Granda just made a noise of contempt, deep in his throat. Otherwise, though, Grandma was as keen on the war effort as we were, collecting in the National Savings every Tuesday morning, knitting comforts for the troops, keeping eggs fresh in Isinglass, and bottling all the fruit she could lay her hands on.

I remember I'd just got home from school that December night. The cottage looked dark and lonely, and my guts scrunched up a bit, as they always did when I passed the checkpoint and said ta-ta to the soldiers, who always called me "Sunny Jim". Granda would still be at work down the fish quay, and Grandma would be finishing her shopping up in Shields. There would be a lot to do: the blackout curtains to draw, the lamps to light (for we had no electricity) and the ready-laid fire to set a match to. Grandma had left some old potatoes in a bowl of water, which meant she wanted me to peel them for supper and put the peelings in the swill-bucket for Mason's pig . . .

I had just lit the last lamp, in the kitchen, and was rolling up my sleeves to tackle the potatoes, when I saw the daddy-long-legs come cruising across the room. It was a big one, a whopper. It looked nearly as big as a German bomber, and I hated it as much. I mean, I love bees and ladybirds, but daddy-long-legs hang about you and suddenly scrape against your bare skin with their scratchy, traily legs. Given half a chance they get down the back of your neck. It was long past the season for them, but this one must have been hibernating or something, and been awakened by a sudden warmth. I backed off, and grabbed an old copy of Granda's *Daily Express* and prepared to swat it. But it had no interest in me. It made straight for the oil-lamp, and banged against the glass shade with that awful persistent pinging. And then suddenly it went down inside, between the shade and the glass chimney. I could still hear it pinging and see its shadow, magnified on the frosted glass. God, it must be getting pretty hot down there . . .

I squinted down cautiously between the shade and the hot chimney. It was hurling itself against the chimney, mad to reach the flame. Silly thing, it would do itself an injury . . . Then I noticed that one of its long crooked legs had already fallen off. As I watched, another broke off. But still the creature hurled itself against the chimney. Another leg went, then another, and there was a stink of burning that was not paraffin. Then it fell against the chimney with a sharp sizzle and lay still at last, just a little dirty mark. There was a tiny wisp of smoke; the stink was awful.

Feeling a bit sick, because it had been a living thing, I went back to peeling the potatoes.

It was then that the siren went. I ran to the door, slipped through the blackout curtain and went outside to look for Granda and Grandma. It was quite dark by that time; but I heard a distant tiny fizz, and the first searchlight came on at the Castle. A dim, poor yellow beam at first, but quickly followed by a brilliant white beam, so bright it looked nearly solid. High up, little wisps of cloud trailed through the beam, like cigarette smoke. Then another beam and another. Four, five, six, all swinging out to seawards, groping for Jerry like the fingers of a robot's hand. Then more, dimmer, searchlights, up towards Blyth. And more still, across the river in South Shields. It made me proud; we were ready for them, waiting.

But in the deep blue reflected light, which lit up the pier road like moonlight, there was no sign of Granda or Grandma. I could see the two sentries on the checkpoint, huddling behind their sandbags, the ends of their fags like little red pin-points. They'd be in trouble for that, if this raid was more than a false alarm. You can see a fag-end from five thousand feet up, my granda says . . .

But otherwise, the pier road was empty. And there was no chance of them coming now; the wardens would force them down some shelter, until the raid was over. I was on my own. I felt a silly impulse to run up and join the sentries, but they'd only send me back into cover. And besides, it was time to be brave. I checked the stirrup-pump with its red buckets of water, in case they dropped incendiaries. Then I did what I was supposed to do, and went down the cellar to shelter.

But there was nothing to do down there. By the light of the oil-lamp, trembling slightly in my hand because it was so heavy, all I could see was Granda's three sacks of spare potatoes, and the dusty rows of Grandma's bottles of elderberry. This year's still had little Christmas balloons, yellow, red and blue, fastened over their necks. They were still fermenting. Some of the balloons were small but fat and shiny; others looked all shrivelled and shrunken.

I should sit down on a mattress and be good. But it was cold and I couldn't hear anything. I mean, the Jerries might be overhead; they might have dropped incendiaries by this time, the cottage roof might be burning, and how would I know? When he was there, in an air-raid, Granda kept nipping upstairs for a look-see. As the person in charge of the cottage tonight, so should I. Or so I told myself.

I crept upstairs. Nothing was on fire. Everything was silent, except for some frantic dog barking on and on, up the town.

And then I heard it; very faint, far out over the sea. *Vroomah, vroomah, vroomah*. Jerry was coming. You could always tell Jerry, because the Raff planes made a steady drone. But Jerry's engines weren't synchronized, Granda said.

And as I went on listening, I knew there was more than one of them. The whole sea was full of their echoes. My stomach drew itself up like a fist. I wasn't scared; just ready. Your stomach always does that.

Then the whole blue scene turned bright pale yellow. The earth shook, and the universe seemed to crack apart like an egg. The Castle guns had fired.

I waited, counting under my breath. Seventeen, eighteen, nineteen. Four brilliant stars out to sea burnt black holes in my eyes. They were in a W-shape, and everywhere I looked now there were four black dots in a W-shape. Then the sound of explosions, rolling in across the water like waves. Then the echoes going away down the coast, off every cliff, fainter and fainter.

The guns fired again. People were rude about those guns. They said they never hit anything; that they couldn't hit a barn-door at ten yards. That the gunners should get their eyes checked. But, tonight . . . There was suddenly a light out to sea, high in the air. A little yellow light where no light should be. The Jerries never showed a light, any more than we did.

But this light grew. And now it was falling, falling. Like a shooting star, when we say that it is the soul of someone dying.

And I knew what it was. We'd hit one. It was going to crash. I leapt up and down in tremendous glee.

Burn, Jerry, burn. We'd had too many folk killed in raids for us to love the Jerries any more.

It never reached the sea. There was such a flash as made the guns look like a piddling Guy Fawkes' night and a bang that hurt my ears. But I could still hear faint cheering – from the Castle, from across the river; very faint, in South Shields. Then there was just a shower of red fragments, falling to the water.

But the rest of the planes came on. The guns went on firing. They were nearly overhead now. There was a faint whispering in the air, then a rattle on the pantiles of Granda's house above me. I ducked down into the cellar entrance. It seemed especially silly to be killed by falling *British* shrapnel . . .

I didn't poke my head out again until it was quiet. Far up the river, the bangs were still lighting up the sky. The red lines of pom-pom tracers climbed so slowly, so lazily. Then the whooshing flicker of the Home Guard's rocket-batteries. And the tremor of the first bombs coming, through the soles of my shoes. It was Newcastle that was copping it tonight . . . we could do with a break.

It was so peaceful, to seawards. Just the faint blue light from the searchlights, which could have been moonlight . . .

And then, by that light, I saw it. White, like a slowly drifting mushroom.

A Jerry parachute. I could see the little black dot of the man, under his harness. He was going to land in the water of the harbour; he was going to get very wet, and that would cool his courage, as Grandma always said. He might drown . . .

The parachute collapsed slowly into the water

about two or three hundred yards out. Ah well, they'd pick him up. The picket-boat on the defence-boom that lay right across the river. It would be full of armed sailors. I was just an interested spectator.

But for some reason, the picket-boat continued to stay moored to the far end of the boom. There was no sound from its heavy diesel engine. Come on, come on! The bloke might drown . . . Or he might come ashore and do anything. Myself, I hoped he drowned.

But I watched and watched, and that boat never stirred. Maybe they hadn't noticed the parachute; maybe they'd been following the raid up the river, like I'd just been doing . . . Maybe the Jerry wasn't drowning; maybe he was swimming ashore at this very moment.

And we were the nearest bit of shore.

I decided to run for the sentries. But at that moment, a second wave of bombers droned in. The shellbursts overhead were churning the sky into a deafening porridge of flashes. I could hear the shrapnel falling, rattling on the roof again. I daren't go out. I'd seen what shrapnel had done to one of Grandpa's rabbits, old Chinnie. I had found her. The roof of her hutch was smashed in, and the floor, and Chinnie lay like a bloody cushion, blue Chinchilla fur hammered into the ground in a mass of wooden splinters and fluff . . .

I hovered piteously from foot to foot. Oh, please God, send him to land somewhere else. South Shields, the rocks below the Castle . . .

I thought at first it was a seal in the water. We get the odd seal up the Gar; they come in for the guts from the fish-gutting, when they're really hungry – even though the Gar is an oily, stinking old river. Sometimes they bob around out there and stare at the land, the water shining on their sleek dark heads.

But seals don't have a pale white blob where their face should be. And seals don't rise up out of the water till their shoulders are showing, then their whole bodies, the gap between their legs. They don't haul themselves out of the water and begin to climb the low soily cliff.

Oh, God, let the guns stop, let the shrapnel stop! But a third wave was vrooming in overhead, and a piece of shrapnel suddenly smashed our front gate into a shower of white fragments.

Suddenly, I made up my mind that I would rather be smashed to a bloody pulp by British shrapnel than be in the power of the Swastika. Holding my arms above my head in an absolutely hopeless attempt to protect myself, I ran for the smashed gate.

As I went through it, a very big, very strong hand grabbed me. I think I squealed like a shot rabbit my father had once had to kill with a blow to the back of the neck. I think I kicked out and bucked wildly, just like that very rabbit, fighting for its life. My efforts were equally useless. The huge hand carried me back to the front door and flung me inside. Our little hall was filled with a huge gasping and panting. Our front door slammed shut. The hand picked me up again and carried me into the living room and threw me on a couch. And for the first time, I saw him.

He was huge, black, shining and dripping water all over Grandma's carpet. He trailed tentacles from his body with little shining metal bits on the end. And he did look like a seal, with the leather helmet almost crushing his head in so that only his eyes showed, and his pale long nose, and his mouth, gaping like a fish's.

"Others?" he shouted. "Others?" He stared around him wildly, then seemed to remember something suddenly and felt, groped at, his shining, dripping side. And pulled out something black with a long tube . . .

I recognized it from the war magazine that my father used to buy me, before he joined the Raff. It was a Luger automatic pistol, with a twelve-shot magazine. All the Jerry aircrew carried them.

He tore off his leather helmet as if it suddenly hurt him. It made him look a bit more human; he had fair hair, quite long, a bit like our Raff types, which

surprised me. Funny how you can still be surprised, even when you're almost wetting yourself with terror . . .

"Others?" he said a third time. He was listening. It made him look like a wild animal, alert. Then I twigged what he was getting at. Was anybody else in the house? Then he grabbed me again, shouting, *"Raus, Raus!"* and dragged me from room to room by my hair.

When we had searched everywhere, even the look-out tower and the cellar, he brought me back and threw me on the couch again. He listened to the outside; the raid had quietened. But he was still shaking. Then he fell into Granda's chair, and we stared at each other. I didn't much like the look of him at all. He had green eyes, too close together.

My Granda always says never to trust a man who has eyes too close together.

Then he pointed the gun at me (I think he enjoyed pointing the gun at me) and said, "Food!"

What could I do but lead him to Grandma's larder? And get him our only half-loaf from the enamel bread-bin. And the butter-dish from the top shelf, with our tiny ration of butter and marge, mixed together so it would last longer. I began to cut a thin slice, but he pushed me aside into a corner with the gun-barrel, then put the gun down and smeared the whole half-loaf with all the butter and marge and began to wolf it down, tearing off huge chunks. I noticed he had very large white teeth, a bit like tombstones. When he had gulped it all down, he poked me into the larder with the gun again, and went along the shelves to see what else he could find. He found our little cheese-ration and swallowed it in one mouthful, just tearing off the greaseproof paper with his large teeth, and swallowing so fast you could tell from the gulp he gave that it hurt him. He found a quarter-jar of jam and began to eat it with a spoon, his gun in his left hand now. Then three shrivelled apples, which he stuffed into a pocket of his dripping suit. Didn't they feed them, before they came on a raid? Were all the Germans starving, like our propaganda used to say, back in the Phoney War?

How did I feel? I felt the end of the world had come, the worst had happened. That I, alone, in Garmouth, was already under the Nazi jackboot. That I was now already inside the Third Reich. He might do anything to me . . .

And yet nothing was changed; the fire still burned on steadily, making steam rise from his suit, as he sat by it. There were Granda's old pipes in their rack, and a twist of tobacco in its silver paper. There was Grandma's knitting still in her chair. The world had turned insane.

And then I began to worry about Granda and Gran. Soon, the raid would be over. Soon they would come walking down the pier road, and straight into . . . Granda might try and do something; he was as brave as a lion. The German would shoot him. Then he might shoot Gran too . . . But what could I do? Nothing. Even when the noise of the raid stopped, there was no point in shouting.

The sentries on the checkpoint would never hear me. And then he would shoot *me* . . .

He was watching me now.

"Derink!" he said. "Derink. Derink!" He made a drinking motion with his free hand.

Like a slave, I crept into the kitchen. A slave of the Third Reich. I got our half-bottle of milk from the cooler on the floor, put it on the kitchen table, and turned to get the tea and sugar canisters and the teapot . . .

"Derink!" he shouted again, and swept them all off on to the floor in his rage. The milk bottle broke and the milk and fragments went everywhere. "Derink!" He raised his hand to his lips again, and threw his head back. I could tell from the shape his fingers made, that he meant he wanted a bottle. He pointed down the cellar. "*Wein . . . vin . . . wine!*"

He must have noticed the row of bottles, Gran's elderberry, when he searched the cellar. I took up the oil-lamp and went down for some. He didn't follow me; only stood by the cellar door, listening to the outside.

The long rows of bottles glistened in the lamplight. They were arranged by year. Gran kept her elderberry a long time . . .

And then it came to me. Gran's elderberry . . . people laughed at it because it wasn't proper wine. But it was strong stuff. She gave the curate from the church a glass of her old batch once, and he liked it so much he'd accepted a second . . .

He was so drunk by the time he reached Front Street that he fell off his bicycle. Elderberry gets stronger every year you keep it. This year's – 1940 – still fermenting, wouldn't do him any harm. But 1939 . . . 1938 . . . I picked up two bottles of her 1938, dusted them with my hand, and carried them upstairs.

He gave a quick, wolfish grin. *"Wein? Ja! Ja!"* He couldn't get a bottle open quick enough. Pulled the cork out with his strong tombstone teeth and spat it out, so it bounced on the hearth-rug. Then he raised the bottle, threw back his head and the sound of glugging filled the room. It was already much more than the curate ever had.

He stopped at last to draw breath. His wolfish grin was wider.

"Wein. Ja. Gut!" He seemed to relax as it hit him.

Stretched his legs out to the fire. Then he had a long think and said, quite clearly but slowly, *"Engländer* not our natural enemy are!"* He seemed quite pleased with himself. Then he took another swig and announced, *"Engländer* little *Brüders* . . . broth . . . brothers are."* He put down the bottle for a moment, and reached out and patted me on the shoulder. Then he picked up the bottle again and offered it to me, indicating that I drink too.

I made a right mess of it. I didn't want to drink, get drunk, and yet I had to. Otherwise he might suspect I was trying to poison him . . .

So I drank, and it went down the wrong way, and I sprayed it all over the place and went into a helpless fit of coughing.

He threw back his head and laughed as if he thought that was hilarious.

"Wein . . . not . . . little *Brüders ist.* Big men . . . *Wein."* He drank some more. The bottle was half-empty by now. The more he got, the more he seemed to want. And, oddly, the better it made his English.

"English little *Brüders* . . . but Europe is corrupt . . . we must make a new order . . . then . . . happy!"

I just waited patiently. Time was on my side now.

It began to have an effect on him. He began to slump deeper into his chair. But the hand with the gun kept playing with it twitchily. I was dead scared it might go off. And he wasn't grinning any more. He looked at me solemnly, owlishly.

"*Prost* . . . drink toast. To Rude! *Mein Kamerad!*" More wine glugged down, while I waited. Then he said, in a small hopeless voice, "Rudi *ist tot* . . . dead. *Und* Karli, *und* Maxi, *und* Heini. *Alles* . . . *tot*."

And then, unbelieving, I saw a tear run down his face. Then another and another. He put his face in his hands and sobbed like a woman, only worse, because women know how to cry properly. He was just a gulping, sniffing, revolting mess. I reckoned that any minute I'd be able to snatch the gun from where it lay. But I didn't know how to use it . . .

"*Kamerad, Kamerad,*" he moaned; comrades, comrades. He was rocking in his chair, like a woman rocking a baby.

And I just waited. Then he began to sing, like a lot of drunks do. Something about *"Ich habe einen Kamerad"*. It was horrible. It embarrassed me so much my toes squirmed inside my shoes.

But I went on waiting.

Finally he stopped, a stupid look of alarm growing on his face. He tried to get up and failed, falling back heavily into the chair. He tried again, pressing down with his hands on the chair-arms. And since he had the bottle in one hand, and the gun in the other, he didn't make it again. The hand holding the bottle opened, and the bottle fell to the rug with a dull clunk and rolled towards me, spilling out a trail of dark elderberry.

Slowly, at last, like a very old man, he managed to lever himself to his feet, and stood swaying above me. I thought he was going to shoot me then. But he decided not to; perhaps he remembered he had sent me for the wine – his little slave-labourer.

Instead, he made a wavering track for the door, crashing into every bit of furniture on the way, hurting himself and gasping. Suddenly he reminded me of something. And I remembered what it was. The daddy-long-legs, in the oil lamp. Like it, he had come flying in; like it, he was dashing himself to bits. I almost laughed out loud. Except that pistol was wavering all over the room.

Then it suddenly went off. Even in the middle of that raid, the noise was deafening. A panel of the door suddenly wasn't there, and the air was full of a Guy Fawkes smell, and the smell of splintered wood. That piney, resinous smell.

Then the gun went off again. He cried out, and I saw blood pouring from a tear in the leg of his wetsuit. And then, with a wild yell, he was out of the front door and the wind was blowing in.

I think I ran across to, of all things, replace the blackout curtain. We were trained so hard to keep the blackout; it was second nature. But as soon as my hand was on it, I heard a yell and a big splash from outside. I knew what had happened. He had fallen into our sandbag-hole – the hole we had thought of using for a duck-pond.

I ran to see. He was just a series of sodden humps, face-down in the water. He didn't move at all. Suddenly a mass of bubbles rose and burst where his face would be, under the water. It was unbelievable. I mean, that hole was only about seven feet across. There wasn't a foot of water in it.

And yet I knew he was drowning. As I watched, one hand came up out of the water and clawed at the side. But it couldn't get a grip, because the sides were steep and slippery. His head turned, his face looked at me and then fell back, and more bubbles came from his mouth.

Soon, any minute now, he would move for the last time; then he would be dead. One dead murderer; one dead Nazi thug.

What made me jump into the hole beside him? Try to lift him out and fail, for he was far too heavy for my eleven years? What made me force my legs under his head and lift his face clear of the filthy, muddy water, so that he could groan and choke and breathe and mutter to himself in a language I would never understand. *"Freund, Freund!"* His big hand wandered round my body, till I grabbed it and held on to it.

"Freund, Freund."

And that was how we stayed, while the returning bombers droned back over us, and the guns fired intermittently, and the shrapnel sang its awful song to earth.

And that was how Granda and Gran found us, and stared at my mud-stained face, after the all-clear had gone. By the light of the fires from the burning docks at Newcastle.

"God love the bairn," said my gran. "What's he doin' wi' that feller?"

Granda took a careful look. "Reckon that feller's a Jerry. Run for the sentries up at the wire, Martha."

I had nothing to say. I was so cold I could not move my jaws any more. But I kept wondering why I did what I did. He was a murderer. Maybe he was the pilot who dropped the bomb that killed my mother at Newcastle, when she'd just nipped down to the shops for a box of matches to light our fire.

That's when my dad joined the Raff. To get revenge.

So why couldn't I just let him lie there and die? I thought a lot about that. It wasn't because he'd ever been nice or likeable; it wasn't even because he'd cried for his dead mates. It wasn't even because if I'd let him die, *I* would have killed him.

It was a heroic thing to kill a Nazi in those days. Everyone would have thought me a hero.

No, it was just that he was still alive. And I didn't want him dead in Granda's garden. I mean, if he'd died, he'd still be there, to me. Even if Granda filled the duck-pond in; which he did, a few days later, shovelling soil from all over the garden into it, furiously. Saying it was a danger in the blackout.

His name was Konrad Huess. I know because he

wrote to me after the war, to thank me. Sent me lots of photos of his wife and kids. I was glad, then. For his wife and kids. But I never replied. I was too mixed-up.

I still am.

ACKNOWLEDGEMENTS

The publishers wish to thank the following for permission to reproduce copyright material:

Theresa Breslin: for "You Can Do It" from *Best of Friends*, Methuen Children's Books Ltd and Mammoth. Copyright © 1995 Theresa Breslin, by permission of Egmont Children's Books Ltd.

John Christopher: for "Dancing Bear" from *The Guardians,* ed. Stephanie Nettell, Penguin Books, 1987, pp. 46-55, by permission of David Higham Associates on behalf of the author.

Helen Dunmore: for "A Gap In The Dark", 1994, by permission of A P Watt Ltd on behalf of the author.

Gerald Durrell: for an extract from "The Reluctant Python" from *A Zoo in my Luggage* by Gerald Durrell, Penguin Books, pp. 30-38. Copyright © 1960 Gerald Durrell, by permission of Curtis Brown Ltd, London on behalf of the estate of the author.

Paul Jennings: for "Batty" from *Undone*, Puffin Books, 1993, pp. 1-17, by permission of Penguin Books Australia Ltd.

Joan Lingard: for "Bicycle Thieves", Methuen, 1989, by permission of David Higham Associates on behalf of the author.

Elisabeth MacIntyre: for "The Unbeliever" from *Eerie Tales,* ed. Margaret Hamilton, 1978, by permission of Hodder and Stoughton Ltd.

Anthony Masters: for "Fixer" from *More of Gary Lineker's Favourite Football Stories*, 1998, by permission of Caroline Sheldon Literary Agency on behalf of the author.

Michael Morpurgo: for an extract from *Waiting for Anya* by Michael Morpurgo, Heinemann, 1990, pp. 54-60, by permission of David Higham Associates on behalf of the author.

Rosemary Sutcliffe: for an extract from *Brother Dusty-Feet*, by Rosemary Sutcliff, Oxford University Press, 1952, pp. 23-33, by permission of David Higham Associates on behalf of the author.

Martin Waddell: for "The Trap" from *Mystery Tour and Other Stories of Detection*, Red Fox Books, 1992, pp. 144-163, by permission of David Higham Associates on behalf of the author.

Robert Westall: for "Daddy-Long-Legs" from *Amazing Adventure Stories*,

ACKNOWLEDGEMENTS

Transworld. Copyright © 1994 the Estate of Robert Westall, by permission of Laura Cecil Literary Agency on behalf of the Estate of the author.

Every effort has been made to trace the copyright holders but where this has not been possible or where any error has been made the publishers will be pleased to make the necessary arrangement at the first opportunity.

More top stories can be found in

Funny Stories for Nine Year Olds

Chosen by Helen Paiba

Hilarious stories include:

The Boy Who Turned Himself Green

Miss Pettigrew's Disappearing Parrot

Doctor Bananas, The Magical Laughter-maker

The Night the Bed Fell Down

Reginald, the Reluctant Dragon

More top stories can be found in

Scary Stories for Nine Year Olds

Chosen by Helen Paiba

Spine-tingling stories include:

The Ghostly Pilot of a Doomed
Plane

The Hitch-hiker Who Never
Reached Home

The Girl in the Mirror

The Dead Hand in the Dark Pool

The Haunting of Nobody House

More top stories can be found in

Animal Stories for TenYear Olds

Chosen by Helen Paiba

Exciting stories include:

The Horse that Saved a Desperate Family

Rex, the Bravest Dog in the World

The Great Elephant Chase

White Fang, the Last Wolf Cub

The Tiger King and the Stupid Snake

More top stories can be found in

Funny Stories for Ten Year Olds

Chosen by Helen Paiba

Hilarious stories include:

Barker, the Millionaire Dog

The Gorilla Who Came to Stay

Sticky Bun and the Sandwich Challenge

Murder by Omelette

The Girl Who Turned into a Penguin

Books in this series available from Macmillan

The prices shown below are correct at the time of going to press. However, Macmillan Publishers reserve the right to show new retail prices on covers which may differ from those previously advertised.

Funny Stories for Ten Year Olds	0 330 39127 5	£3.99
Scary Stories for Ten Year Olds	0 330 39126 7	£3.99
Animal Stories for Ten Year Olds	0 330 39128 3	£3.99
Adventure Stories for Eight Year Olds	0 330 39140 2	£3.99
Funny Stories for Nine Year Olds	0 330 37491 5	£3.99
Scary Stories for Nine Year Olds	0 330 37492 3	£3.99
Animal Stories for Nine Year Olds	0 330 37493 1	£3.99
Adventure Stories for Nine Year Olds	0 330 39141 0	£3.99
Funny Stories for Eight Year Olds	0 330 34946 5	£3.99
Scary Stories for Eight Year Olds	0 330 34944 9	£3.99
Animal Stories for Eight Year Olds	0 330 35495 7	£3.99
Adventure Stories for Eight Year Olds	0 330 39140 2	£3.99

All Macmillan titles can be ordered at your local bookshop

or are available by post from:

**Book Service by Post
PO Box 29, Douglas, Isle of Man IM99 1BQ**

Credit cards accepted. For details:
Telephone: 01624 675137
Fax: 01624 670923
E-mail: bookshop@enterprise.net

Free postage and packing in the UK.
Overseas customers: add £1 per book (paperback)
and £3 per book (hardback).

MELLIN DE SAINT-GELAIS AND LITERARY HISTORY

FRENCH FORUM MONOGRAPHS

47

Editors R.C. LA CHARITÉ and V.A. LA CHARITÉ

The publication of this book was subsidized in part by the Solomon Lincoln Fund of the Department of Romance Languages and Literatures, Harvard University.